CHAOS

NOMAD SERIES – BOOK 4

K.A.FINN

Also by K. A. Finn

Nomad Series (Space Opera)

Ares

Nemesis

Perses

Chaos

Mania

Talon (TBA)

Broken Chords (Rockstar Romance)

Broken Rock

Fractured Rock

Split Rock (2023)

Crushed Rock (TBA)

Shattered Rock (TBA)

Blackjacks (Paranormal Romance)

Breaking Phoenix

Reviving Davyn

Defying Shep (TBA)

Unraveling Fallon (TBA)

A bit of a Nomad herself, **K.A. Finn** has wandered around Ireland and the UK for decades before settling back in Ireland with her husband and kids (two and four legged).

Visit K.A. Finn online:

www.kafinn.com
(trailers, excerpts, artwork, playlists etc)

Facebook: kafinnauthor

Instagram: kafinnauthor

Twitter @K_A_Finn

Coming next

MANIA

Nomad Series Book 5

Cover design by Deranged Doctor Design

Published by Cooper Publishing

www.cooperbookservices.com

Edited by Desert Mystic Literary Editing

www.desertmysticliteraryediting.com

ISBN: 978-1-914177-33-0

First Edition: October 2020

To my girls and the endless, fun filled *chaos*
they bring to my life

CHAOS

NOMAD SERIES – BOOK 4

K.A.FINN

PART 1

DAEGAN/GRYFFIN — 10 YEARS OLD

BRAY — 5 YEARS OLD

PROLOGUE

EARTH

Maggie Sawyer closes the small bag and places it on the bed beside her. She watches Daegan pack his wash bag as Brayden plays on the floor. She smiles when he ignores the hairbrush by the sink and closes the bag. She's not surprised he didn't pack it. Brushing his unruly locks is a daily battle - one she will miss for the next week. The school trip to the planetarium wasn't mandatory, but against her better judgement, she caved and signed the permission note.

'Brush, Daegan.'

He gives her his best stern glare. 'But Mom-'

'Not another word.'

He sighs dramatically and slams his bag back on the sink.

'Hairbrush again.'

She smiles at her brother Morgan as he steps into the room. He bends down and ruffles Bray's hair. 'How did you guess?'

'It'll pass. In a few years, he'll be chasing the ladies. He'll want to look his best for that.'

'He's only ten. Can we please keep ladies off his radar for the moment?'

Morgan laughs and gestures to the bag on the floor. 'You finished with your bag, Daegan?'

Daegan throws his wash bag into the backpack and fastens it. 'Yep. All done.'

Morgan takes the bag and Maggie holds out her hands. Bray eagerly grabs her fingers while Daegan looks at her for a few seconds before giving in. She keeps hold of her sons' hands as they walk down the path to the waiting transport. As soon as Daegan sees the transport he tries to pull his hand out of her grip, but she keeps a firm hold. Morgan packs his bag into the cargo compartment then comes back to stop Bray from running into the waiting vehicle.

Maggie crouches down and pushes a particularly stubborn lock of hair from Daegan's eyes. 'Best behaviour, Daegan. Do as you're told, finish your meals and go to bed on time. No messing. Do you hear me?'

'I already said I'd behave.'

'I know you did, but you don't always listen to me.' She nearly adds that he's as stubborn as his father but stops herself in time. He knows he has a different father to Bray, but she hasn't found the right time to tell him about Roman. Admitting the truth to Daegan would force her to have a similar discussion with

Roman. She's not quite ready to explain why she had kept his son a secret for a decade. Pushing thoughts of the dark haired Foundation officer from her mind is easier said than done. Daegan is so much like his father, and not just in his looks. His obsession with getting among the stars could only have come from Roman. She pushes Roman to the back of her mind and smiles at his son. 'I'm your Mom. It's my job to repeat myself.'

He glances at the transport then back at her. 'Can I go now?'

'In a minute.' She unclips the pendant from around her neck and holds it out to him. The small platinum griffin sways in the breeze, the sun glinting off the small creature. Roman had given it to her a few weeks before she broke his heart and he left Earth for a new life. 'I want you to wear this.'

'Mom...'

'Humour me, okay.' She fastens it around his neck and he quickly buries it under his t-shirt. 'You leave that on. It'll keep an eye on you until you come home to me. Promise me you won't take it off, Daegan.'

He sighs dramatically, his attention on the transport and his friends. 'I promise. Can I go now?'

She nods, knowing he's more interested in the transport than anything she has to say. 'Of course. Say goodbye to your brother.'

He gives Bray a brief hug, pushing his younger brother away when he tries to latch on. Before he can escape, Maggie embraces him, holding him tightly. He hugs her back then squirms out of her arms. He grabs his backpack, races down the driveway, and disappears into the transport. He sits at the back with one of his friends and waves out the window as the transport pulls away.

Morgan drapes his arms over her shoulder while keeping a wriggling Bray secure in his other arm. 'Hey, you okay?'

'I know Dean and I leave them every few weeks, but this time is different. He's leaving, not us.'

'Daegan is ten going on twenty. He's well overdue a few nights away from home.'

'He's going off-world Morgan, not camping in the woods.'

'On a highly organised school trip. Stop worrying. He'll have a ball and come back in a week with loads of stories. Now, I'm going to get this little man some lunch. You coming?'

'I'll be there in a minute.' Bray waves at her over Morgan's shoulder as he's taken into the house. Maggie looks back down the drive. She knows Morgan is right. The school has visited the planetarium numerous times without any issues. That doesn't help to quell her uneasiness. She can't explain why, but all she wants to do is chase after the transport and bring Daegan back home. She pulls herself away from the driveway and follows Morgan into the house. It's going to be a long week. She knows she won't relax until she holds Daegan in her arms again.

PART 2

5 YEARS LATER

GRYFFIN — 15 YEARS OLD
BRAY — 10 YEARS OLD

1

Rayde, Captain of the Nomad flagship, *Ares*, rises from his seat and looks out the front of the ship. 'Well? Where the hell is he?'

His first officer, Creed, shakes his head. The young man had been on board *Ares* since he was fifteen-years-old. Even at that young age, he had proved himself time and time again. When Rayde's old first officer was killed in a slaver attack, it made sense to promote Creed to the position even though he was a mere twenty-five-years-old. It was a decision he had never regretted. 'No idea, sir.'

Their contact had a habit of being late. 'Check the

coordinates again.'

Creed taps at the screen then curses. 'The fucking idiot. He's about an hour away. Gave us the wrong coordinates.'

'Tell him we're on the way but I'm knocking ten thousand credits from our payment.'

'Sir, I'm picking up a faint signal. There's something out here.'

'Might as well check it out. I'd prefer this wasn't a wasted trip.'

Creed moves *Ares* towards the signal and ten minutes later they find the source. Rayde zooms in on the image on the viewscreen. 'What the hell is a station doing out here? Any ID codes?'

'Nothing, sir. Minimal life support in some areas but apart from that, she's dead.'

Rayde considers passing by. The station barely looks like it would withstand a boarding party, let alone hold anything of value to them. He is about to issue the order to move on when he has second thoughts. The last few weeks have been one dog-fight after another with Rogue groups. The ship needed repairs as did the crew. If they could salvage parts and, although highly unlikely, provisions, it was worth a look. 'I want three teams suited up and ready to go in five minutes. Let's see what she has to offer.'

He makes his way down to the airlock and widens his stance to balance himself as *Ares* locks into position at one of the station's docking bays. He checks the oxygen levels on his mask then looks at the rest of the team for confirmation their masks are working before he opens the airlock. Taking the lead, Rayde steps through the hatch and onto the station. His skin immediately chills. He can't explain it but there's something seriously off with the station. He looks down at his levels and, seeing the air is breathable, removes his mask for a few seconds. After a lungful of rancid air he changes his mind. Life support may be working in this area but the foul-smelling air is enough to turn his stomach. 'Keep your masks on and your eyes open, men. There are corpses around here somewhere.'

The teams split up and Rayde follows the main corridor to the centre of the station. They check every room they pass but each one is empty. Not even any scrap metal worth taking. Finally, he enters a large, circular room in the centre of the station. Rayde has witnessed many battles in his career, but the scene in front of him is too much even for him. He hears one of his men emptying his stomach behind him and he can't blame him.

Blinking lights in the ceiling cast an eerie glow on a room he knows will haunt his nightmares. A row of large rusted cages lines the far wall, each one with a decomposing corpse chained inside. Bloodstained restraints hang from the metal table sitting in the centre over a foul-smelling drain. As much as he wants to turn tail and run back to *Ares*, he convinces his legs to move him further into the room past half a dozen tables laden with medical instruments and other unrecognisable metal components. As with the operating table, everything is stained with dried blood. Behind the tables, an empty desk is covered with trailing wires and a cracked screen. 'Looks like someone left in a hurry. Took the units with them.'

'I could do with leaving in a hurry,' Creed says. 'Something seriously wrong went on here.'

'Agreed. Check there's nothing of value left then get the hell out of here. This place gives me the creeps.'

He leaves Creed to search the far side of the room with his team and goes over to examine some of the cages. Fifteen of the twenty cages are occupied. Judging by the state of the bodies, they've been dead for anywhere from a few weeks to a few years. The light on his gun passes over each of the bodies in turn. They're small. Too damn small to have found their end in this place. 'We're too late to help these poor creatures.'

'I know,' Creed replies. 'I can smell them. There's nothing worth taking either.'

'Clear out.' He turns back towards the door, eager to get back to *Ares* and a stiff drink. His torchlight catches something on the floor near the far wall. He moves closer and finds another body. A heavy chain connects the metal collar around the boy's neck to a sturdy bolt on the wall. Unlike the others, this one is a recent fatality. The boy is young, early teens at the most. Rayde crouches down to get a better look and frowns. 'This body has metal attached to it.'

Creed appears at his side and looks down at the boy.

'That's wrong. What the hell went on in this place?'

'Nothing good.' Rayde pushes to his feet and turns away from the body. He takes a step towards the door and stumbles, catching himself before he lands on the filthy floor.

'Sir?'

'Tripped on something.' He directs his torch at the floor and frowns when he sees what caught his foot. The boy's arm is stretched out in front of him. 'His arm wasn't there a second ago, right?'

Creed shrugs.

Rayde crouches down again and touches the boy's shoulder. He gently rolls him onto his back and freezes. The boy is looking at him. As he stares, the boy blinks slowly. 'Creed!'

Creed looks down and curses. 'He's alive?'

'Get something to cut this chain off him.'

Creed hurries over to one of the tables of instruments and returns with a large cutter. He cuts the chain attached to the boy's collar as Rayde removes his coat. He drapes it over the boy, tucking it around his skeletal body. 'Time to get you out of here, son. I'm going to lift you, okay?'

He gets no response so he directs his torch at the boy again. Rayde frowns as something catches his torchlight. A pendant has slipped out from under the loose-fitting collar. The creature is unfamiliar to him, it's wings, claws and beak those of a bird but clearly there are other beasts mixed with it. Dismissing it, Rayde slips his arms under the boy and rises to his feet. He's carried heavier weapons. He adjusts his grip, trying not to hurt him, but the boy is out of it. Creed leads the way out of the room while Rayde follows, checking for yet more unpleasant surprises. He forces himself to walk slowly even though he wants to run off this station. He's not the most law-abiding of men, but even he knows wrong when he sees it. Everything about this place is wrong. It gives him the creeps and he's not afraid to admit it.

Finally, he turns the corner and sees the airlock leading to safety. Creed picks up the pace. He must want to get off the station as much as Rayde does.

Rayde leaves his mask on as he hurries through *Ares'* cramped corridors, never so glad to be back on board as he is right now. He lays the boy on a bed in the med bay and steps back to get a proper look in the light. Ryder, the ships medic, grabs a med kit and freezes when he sees what Rayde's brought him. 'What the hell?'

Rayde agrees but can't find words to describe what's lying on the bed. The boy is tall but incredibly thin. His dark hair is long and matted and every one of his bones is visible. He can handle that. It's the metal fixed to him that he's having trouble understanding. Crude metal components similar to the ones Rayde saw at the station are screwed onto his face, neck, back, chest, and legs. His right arm is missing halfway between the wrist and elbow joint and is tipped with what looks like metal connectors. What isn't mutilated with metal is badly scarred under layers of filth and dried blood. 'Can you help him?'

Ryder stares at Rayde. 'Help him? How? I wouldn't know where to start. Hell, I don't even know what I'm looking at. You sure he's alive?'

'He grabbed my leg and blinked. His chest is moving too. Don't think he'll hang around for long so can you try to do something.'

Ryder blows out a long breath as he stares down at the boy. 'Is there anything on the station that'll hint at what was done to him?'

'I'll get some teams back to the station to see if we can find anything.'

'That'd help. For the moment, all I can do is clean him up, see to the wounds I can, and make him comfortable. If he survives we can deal with the rest.'

'Creed, take a team back to the station. Bring back anything that looks similar to what he has on him.' Rayde leans closer to the boy's face. 'What did you do to deserve this, son, eh?'

Ryder pulls on a pair of gloves. 'I wouldn't hold your breath for an answer, sir. Can't see him pulling through.'

'You all packed?'

Maggie smiles at Dean and nods. 'That's the last of them on the floor.'

Bray walks downstairs with his parents and follows them out to the transport. His father loads the final bag in the back and gestures to the field beside the lake.

'How about a walk before we head off?'

Bray kicks at the short stubble covering the field. His uncle, Morgan, had taken a crop of straw off it a week ago.

Dean leads them over to the large tree by the edge

of the lake and they sit. 'So, buddy. You know why we have to go?'

Bray nods. 'Yep. You're going to bring Daegan back. Do you think you'll be back for his birthday?'

Maggie smiles. 'I hope so, Bray. We're going to do everything we can to bring him home, but we might not be able to find him.'

'You will. Shayla said she'll help me make him a cake. Do you think he still likes spaceships?'

Dean shuffles around to face his son. 'It's good you're staying positive. We all have to, but I don't want you to get your hopes up.'

'I'm not. You've already said all this to me.'

'I know we have,' Maggie says. She pulls him close to her and rests her chin on his head. 'Your dad and I will look harder than anyone has ever looked for someone before. I promise you. We all want him back so bad. You need your big brother around so he can boss you.'

Bray snorts. 'Erin does that.'

'You give as good as you get, buddy,' his father says, laughing. 'Just try to ease off while we're gone, okay? Morgan and Shayla don't need any cheek from you.'

Bray holds up his hand and put on the most innocent look he can. 'I swear I'll be super good and not boss Erin around.'

Dean and Maggie laugh, clearly not fooled by his declaration. 'Yeah right. You honestly expect us to believe that.' Dean gets up and holds out his hand. 'C'mon. Time we get going.'

Bray laughs as his dad pulls him quickly to his feet. Dean smirks and starts running towards the house. 'Five credits I win.'

'Hey! You cheated,' Bray shouts then takes off across the field after him. They catch up with each other at the gate and Bray tugs at his father as he tries to climb over. Dean falls to the ground and Bray launches himself on top of him. Dean laughs and stops struggling. 'Fine! You win.'

'I always win.'

'Why do you think I always cheat? I need to get some kind of advantage.'

They brush themselves off as Maggie joins them. She brushes straw from Bray's hair and hugs him to her again. 'Aren't you forgetting something?'

'Oh yeah,' he exclaims with a grin. He holds out his hand. 'That'll be five credits, please.'

Dean mutters under his breath but pulls the credits out of his pocket. 'Serves me right I guess. Okay, time we head out I think.'

They walk back to the transport and say their goodbyes. Maggie wraps her arms around her son. 'We'll be back in a few weeks, okay?'

'With Daegan.'

She smiles. 'I hope so.'

Bray stands beside Shayla, Morgan, and Erin as they wave at the transport moving down the driveway. As soon as it disappears around the corner Bray hurries inside the house and up the stairs. 'Hey! Where you off to?' Morgan shouts after him.

'To clean my room. Daegan hasn't seen it for five years. I want it tidy.' Too excited about possibly seeing his big brother again, he misses the look that passes between his aunt and uncle. He probably would have ignored it anyway. They keep telling him not to get carried away but this is a big deal. In a few weeks he could have his family back again.

ARES

Rayde looks up from his unit when he hears a knock on the door. 'Yeah.' Creed strolls into the room with Ryder. Both men drop into the chairs in front of Rayde looking pale and tired. 'How are you getting on?'

Creed makes a face as he stuffs his hands into his pockets. 'I'm getting myself a drink when I'm done here - I can promise you that.'

'Is the boy still alive?'

Ryder nods. 'Well, he's breathing and he's got a pulse. Not sure that's a good thing for the lad.'

'What do you mean?' Rayde asks as he pushes back in his chair.

'Well, apart from the obvious malnutrition and dehydration which could easily finish him off, he's got a nasty infection in what's left of that arm of his. I reckon the metal tip will have to come off so we can amputate another few inches. From what I can make out, the metal on his face is linked to his brain so there's no removing that. Same with the piece on his chest and his organs. The bits on his neck and legs could probably be taken off, but I haven't got a clue how. He's also... well, he's been up close and personal with a knife... you know... down there.' Ryder gestures to his groin and winces. 'It looks nasty but I don't reckon it'll do him any harm long term. Well, unless he's planning on having kids.'

Rayde's eyebrows rise at the news. 'I think that's the least of his issues right now.'

'Couldn't agree more. I should also be able to cut the collar off him. I'll do that before he wakes up - if he wakes up. I've shaved his head. I won't tell you what was living in his hair. He's had a good wash too. Sir, I'll do what I can for the fellow, but I'm going to need help with the metalwork. We were able to use one of the scanners from the station to get a better look at the internal ones. Seems like they're cloaked or shielded or something like that. Anyway, there's so much wiring and metalwork in him it's way beyond me.'

Rayde turns his attention to Creed. 'Any luck getting anything useful from the station?'

'We've taken all the metal that looks like what he has on him. We've also managed to find an old unit in a storage room off the lab. Hopefully, it'll have something that will explain what the hell was going on in that place.'

'Not sure I want to know,' Rayde mutters. 'Any idea how long he's been there for?'

'Creed described the other bodies. I'd guess about five years or so. It's hard to put an age on him but maybe mid-teens. He's also got a number on the back of his left shoulder. Looks like an ID mark of some sort. Whatever was going on there, he was number thirty-five. Damn thing was burnt into his skin. By the look of the scarring, it's been there a few years.'

Creed grimaces. 'Nice. I'm loving that place more by the second. I'll check what we took from the station. See if I can find a reference to that number. Looks like we just missed whoever was running this place. They cleared out two days ago. One of the rooms was being lived in. It was a man. Few shirts and trousers. Nothing we could ID him from though. System says the airlock was opened two days ago. Nothing else till we docked.'

'He left the boy like that?'

'Nothing about that place would surprise me,' Creed says. 'It needs to be destroyed.'

'Agreed. Clear everyone off the station and make sure it's history. Signal when you're ready. We'll give them the respect they deserve. It's about time those poor beings had a proper burial.'

'Gladly, sir.'

'Ryder, do what you can for the boy. Make him

comfortable. I'll try and track down someone that can help.'

'There's a good chance he'll die, sir.'

Rayde nods. 'I know. Nomads don't leave people behind, Ryder. He deserves to live after having to spend even a day in that place.'

'I get that. Thing is, even if he does make it, he's not going to be… right.'

'What do you mean?'

'Rayde, he's been mistreated for years. Lack of food and water would have been enough to cause him issues, but he might have seen the others go. Who knows how many times he was on that table or what was done to him. As I said, he may not be right.' Ryder taps the side of his head with a long finger. 'Up there, sir.'

'Understood,' Rayde replies. 'Do what you can.'

Ryder leaves and Rayde wipes a hand over his face. He messed up by taking the boy off the station. What he should have done is put a bullet in his head and left him there. From what he just heard he hasn't done him any favours. The kid will be in for a long and painful recovery – if he survives.

If he had been a few years older or even younger, he probably would have done just that. Rayde pours himself a drink and empties the glass. Why did he have to be the same age as Tris? He never knew his son. Hell, he didn't even know he had one until he was told he died. He was with the mother once and Tris was the result. Not that she told him. Damn woman had kept it from him. Wouldn't have made a difference if she did tell him. He never wanted kids. Had no interest in them.

His sixteen-year-old son died a year ago. Some issue with his heart. Guilt wasn't something Rayde indulged in too often, but it had hit him like a gunshot to the gut on the station. For some reason, seeing that boy threw him off balance. His son would have been the same age as the boy. His son died without knowing him, without knowing who he is or what he does. His heir died without knowing what his father had achieved. Maybe this boy is his second chance at that legacy. Someone to carry on his ways, his rules after he was gone. He fills his glass again and sips it this time. He could mould this boy into someone worthy of the honour. At a time of Rayde's choosing of course.

4

The young boy lies in the corner of the room, listening to the sounds around him. He thinks he's on a ship - there's a vibration that wasn't on the station. The air smells strange too. Very different to the station. He's not sure if it's better or worse - just different. It doesn't make his stomach churn. Maybe that is better.

He scratches at the strip of material around his arm. He can feel the familiar pull of stitches in the skin under the material. The Scientist never used anything to cover the cuts he made. The material is better than being able to see the cuts on his body. He never wants to see them again.

He's not sure how much time has passed since he woke up in this strange place. His new owners have been kind to him so far, but that would change. The Scientist had made sure to tell him every day how no one wanted him, no one cared about him. His new owners may have cut the collar off, set his bones, bandaged his cuts and fed him, but that didn't mean he would let his guard down.

A part of him hopes things will be different with these owners. Maybe they won't hurt him as the Scientist had. Maybe he'd... He closes his eyes and suppresses a shiver. He wouldn't let himself get carried away. He learnt that lesson within a few minutes of arriving at the station.

When their ship was attacked he had thought he was scared. He can't escape the sound of gunfire hitting the hull, the complete blackness as the ship died, the screams of his friends when the intruders had burst into their rooms and pulled them out one by one, and thrown them onto another ship. He thought things couldn't get more terrifying, but he was wrong. Hearing the first screams from the table in the centre of the room had scared him more than anything else he can remember. Being here, on this strange ship doesn't scare him. Nothing is scary after where he'd just been.

His breath hitches in his throat. Unless the Scientist is here too. What if he had abandoned the station and was using this ship instead? He glances over at the plate of food beside him. The Scientist never fed him on a plate. He always threw leftovers on the floor. The food he had been given here was clean and tasted better than anything he can remember.

He allows himself to relax a little. He doesn't think the Scientist is here. Maybe he's finally escaped.

The door opens and the boy melts further into the corner, trying to make himself as small as possible. He's not scared, just wary. He tucks his head under his arms and peers through a small gap at the man in front of him. It's the large man who was there when he woke up.

'How are you feeling today, son?'

The boy silently watches his new owner as he places a fresh tray of food on the floor in front of him. The man joins him on the ground and passes him a piece of bread. The boy eyes the food suspiciously.

'Have you found your voice yet?'

The boy remains silent. The man places the bread back on the plate and pushes it closer but he doesn't move to take it. He'll wait until the other man is gone.

'We should be able to remove some of those implants in a few days when you're a little stronger. Looks like I've been able to track down someone who can pull together an arm for you too. One that we can adapt as you grow. How does that sound?'

The boy thinks it sounds good. He looks down at the lump of metal sticking out of his arm. It hurts. Everything hurts. The man had been able to take some of the pain away, but not enough. Not yet.

'So, do you remember your name?'

He doesn't. Ever since his parents sold him to the Scientist he had been called Thirty-Five. He's not sure but he doesn't think that's his actual name.

The man nods and takes a piece of bread from the plate and pops it in his mouth. He looks over at the boy and points to the pendant around his neck. 'That bird thing was tucked under that collar you were wearing. I did some searching. It's called a griffin.'

The word means nothing to the boy. He knows the small animal on the ragged piece of string is important but he can't remember why. Until the man cut his collar off, he had forgotten all about it.

'We need to call you something.' He scratches his jaw then snaps his fingers, startling the boy. 'How about this? Until you remember your real name, we'll call you Gryffin. Is that okay?'

The boy likes that. It's better than being called Thirty-Five. He never wants to be called that again. He cautiously reaches out and snatches the piece of bread from the tray. The man smiles at him. 'That's it, Gryffin. Eat up. You need a fair bit of meat on those bones of yours. We've got a long journey ahead. It's not going to be easy for you, but I promise I'll be with you every step of the way. I'm going to do everything I can to help you fulfil your potential.'

Gryffin manages a small smile. He doesn't want to trust this man, but maybe he's telling the truth. Maybe this will be an end to all the hurt, and the cold, and the dark. Maybe this man will help him. Maybe he'll be able to stop the pain.

OFF-GRID MEDICAL CENTRE

The woman pushes her grey hair back from her face and covers her mouth with her hand. Rayde can't say he blames her. Even cleaned up and bandaged, Gryffin isn't going to win any beauty contests. Creed leans against the wall to block unwanted guests from crashing their party. His eyes keep wandering over to Gryffin. He'd been as surprised as anyone when the boy had survived the first night, and the second, and the third.

The woman walks around Gryffin, her eyes taking in every inch of his scrawny form. He's wearing the smallest shirt they could find onboard, which hangs off his bony frame like an ill-fitting sack. As the woman makes her visual examination, Rayde finds himself impressed by Gryffin's reaction. When they had rescued him from the station, he assumed he was weak and timid. Looking at him now he is slowly realising that underneath, he is far from weak. Even after a few days of food and medical care, he has improved greatly. He's as far from a credible threat as you can be but stands tall as he quietly stares at the strange woman. He must be wary and perhaps scared about the situation but isn't showing it.

'What am I looking at?' the woman mumbles as she comes to a stop in front of Gryffin again.

'As I said in my message, he needs this metalwork looked at. New arm too if possible.'

She waves her hand in the air in front of Gryffin. 'Yes, yes, yes, but what is he? Did you do this?'

Rayde moves over to the woman and crosses his arms. 'What the hell are you talking about? He's a boy who needs an arm and some medical attention. That's all you need to know.' He nods over to Creed who pulls a bag from his shoulder. He lays it on the table and opens it. He lifts three mechanical arms from the bag then steps back to the door. 'We found those with him. As you can see, they're far too small for him. Are you able to modify them? Make them fit better?'

The woman looks from the arms to Gryffin then back to the arms. She examines the arms and something changes in her face and stance that he's not entirely comfortable with. 'This metal isn't cheap. Not found around these parts. Where'd you get it from?'

'Do I look like I'm here for a chat? See to the boy or we find someone who will.'

She snorts and slams the arm back on the table. 'Twenty-five thousand credits. Beforehand mind you. I don't take IOU's.'

'Half now. Half when you're done.'

She mutters some choice words under her breath then nods. 'Deal.'

Creed hands her a pouch and she turns away to count the credits. 'Very well.' She gestures to the door behind them. 'Get him up on the table. I'll need to examine him before I start.'

Like a switch, Rayde could swear the temperature in the room plummets. He looks over at Gryffin. The boy's entire demeanour has changed. He slowly shakes his head and takes a step back, bumping into Creed. Gryffin folds into a ball on the floor. He wraps his arm around his knees and rocks back and forth, shaking his head over and over.

Rayde gestures to the woman. 'Get your things ready.' She wanders into the adjoining room. 'Creed. You stick with her. I'd trust a slaver before I'd trust her. The way she's talking about his metalwork. I don't like it. We need her alive though - for now.'

He waits until Creed leaves before crouching down to join Gryffin on the floor. Up close he can see the tremors working through the boy's body. 'Hey. You going to tell me what's up?'

He knows he's not going to get an answer but he's

going to keep trying.

'I told you I'm going to watch your back. I meant that. Creed and I will be watching her and will kill her if she does anything we're not happy with. You're safe with us, Gryffin. I promise.'

With a bit more gentle persuasion, he finally lets Rayde lead him into the adjoining room. It's a far cry from the lab he found the boy in but Gryffin is far from happy about being there. Can't blame him. He doubts he'd be all too keen about it himself.

Rayde guides Gryffin to the table and helps him slide onto it. Gryffin takes off his t-shirt and lies down but looks like he's about to bolt from the room. He intently focuses on the woman who in turn is intently examining him. She leans closer and prods at the implant on his chest. 'Interesting. Same unique metal. Very interesting. Right, well I'll have to scan all this stuff and see what we're working with.'

Creed hands her the scanner they found on the station. 'He's shielded from scans. This is the only one that works.'

'Is that so? Nothing strange about that at all.'

She grabs the scanner from Creed and hooks it into her system. Gryffin keeps his attention on the woman as she passes the scanner over his body, making tutting and grunting noises as she goes.

Eventually, she stands up and looks at her archaic system. 'This is some seriously disturbing stuff.'

'Do you know what it is?'

She snorts and throws a withering look at Rayde.

'Of course I know what it is. It's cybernetics. This is the first cyborg I've seen. Not the best example if you ask me. These implants have been fitted to improve or enhance what's already there. They'll need all the help they can get.'

'Can any of them be removed?'

She grunts and examines the data again before nodding. She jabs a finger at Gryffin's neck. 'This piece hasn't been activated. There's one on his back and the pieces on his legs. All that can go. The rest he's stuck with. Part of him now.'

'Damn it,' Rayde mutters. 'Nothing at all you can do?'

'You asked my opinion, Nomad. Least you can do is not argue with me. I'm sure! The one around his eye is screwed to his skull. It links with an extensive implant on his brain. Looks to be a master or control implant. Don't fancy his odds if I go meddling in there. The chest one seems to regulate the others.'

'Others? You mean his arm.'

'No, I mean the other implants.' She turns the screen around and Rayde sees what she's talking about. Highlighted on the screen are dozens of implants throughout his body.

'Why couldn't we see that?'

She shrugs. 'This machine was top of the range when I got it. Your system probably wasn't designed for this sort of scanning. Anyway, he's riddled with the things. No getting them out. The chest piece needs rework. A section of it is damaged. Without it he's dead.'

'Best you get to work then.'

The woman hands Rayde a syringe. 'Knock him out.'

Rayde leans over Gryffin and smiles. 'This'll put you to sleep for a bit. When you wake up you'll be sorted. I promise.'

Gryffin frowns then closes his eyes and takes a deep breath. The calm acceptance is disturbing Rayde more than he'd like to admit. The whole fucking situation is giving him the creeps. The way Gryffin is acting tells Rayde he's been in a situation like this before and knows what's about to happen. The boy has accepted – rightly or wrongly – that there's nothing he can do to stop what's about to happen. There's no point fighting cause it won't change a damn thing.

He licks his dry lips and looks down at the syringe in his hand. Maybe the fucker who did this to the boy and the others in the lab didn't bother with knocking them out before he torn them apart. Sick bastard.

Gryffin looks up at him as he injects the sedative into his neck. The boy's frown slowly fades as he succumbs to the effects of the drug. The doctor takes a screwdriver from the table next to her and sets to work on the thick implant on his neck. Rayde watches in morbid fascination as she unscrews the metal from the boy's flesh. She holds out a screw and drops it into Rayde's hand. He stares at the screw, horrified by the size of the thing. Three fixings later, she slowly pries the metal from Gryffin's neck and places the implant on the table. 'It's left a nasty wound.' She rummages in a drawer next to her and takes out a sealed container. The woman peels the cover off and lifts a gelatinous strip from inside. She positions it over the wound and presses it down. 'Acts like a graft. It'll protect the wound from infection while it heals. The graft will absorb into his skin after a few weeks. Shouldn't leave much of a scar. Now, let's see what's going on with his chest.'

She removes a piece of the chest plate and grunts. 'Wiring is decent. Should last him another few years.' She passes the scanner over his chest and points to the screen. 'See that? The bit you see on the outside is just a cover. Everything that's controlling the implants is deeper inside him. The casing is sealed. Makes it waterproof. Wouldn't want the internal wiring getting too wet so make sure the plating is well maintained. I'll fit some ports you can connect monitors to. You should check the programming regularly. That fails and he's dead.'

'Can you tell how long he's had these for?'

She scrunches up her face. 'Three to six years I'm guessing. His eye is newer than the chest plate.'

'His eye?'

'The one with the metal around it has artificial innards. Rest is his own.' She fits the cover back on the chest plate and screws the pieces in place before moving to the connector covering the tip of his arm. 'Don't need to tell you that arm is rotten. Haven't seen an infection that bad in years. Nasty. I'll have to remove the connector and take more of his arm. Up to his elbow should be enough.'

'Whatever you have to do.'

The woman begins removing the connector pieces, carefully stripping it back so she can rebuild and refit it later. Once all the visible parts are off and being thoroughly disinfected, she turns her attention to the mess of his lower arm. As soon as she begins working, Gryffin opens his eyes and tries to scramble off the table, knocking the tray of instruments on the floor.

'I thought you'd sedated him?'

The woman checks the syringe. 'He got the full dose. He should be out for hours! What the hell is going on?'

Rayde ignores her screeching and leans over Gryffin. 'Hey. Calm down! It's okay. You're safe. Look at your arm, son. It's in a bad way. She can help you but it means removing that infected part. Once she does that we'll be able to get you a new arm.'

Gryffin looks down at his discoloured stump and his breathing slows. He lies back on the table and holds his arm out to the woman.

Creed storms over to the woman, pinning her to the edge of the table with his body. 'He wants you to fix him.'

'Not a chance! I'm not risking my life. What if it attacks me?'

'Give him more sedative.'

'The dose I gave him will knock out most people for hours. Not my fault that thing isn't affected.'

'Give him as much as it takes to keep him under.'

She sneers down at Gryffin. 'It could kill it.'

'Stop calling him 'it' or it won't just be him you have to keep an eye on. Now, get back to work so you can get your money. I'll watch his vitals. You do what you need to with that arm. You get me?'

'I'll want double for this, mind you.'

'Fine. Just finish this.'

With another dose in him, Gryffin stills on the table. As soon as she makes the first incision his eyes open again, but the increased dosage keeps him groggy and disorientated. 'Hey, You doing okay, son?'

Gryffin looks at him then closes his eyes again.

'Keep going. He doesn't seem to be in pain.'

'Or he wants that arm fixed and he's doing a damn good job hiding the pain,' Creed mutters.

The doctor continues as Gryffin drifts in and out of consciousness. Rayde doesn't know what disturbs him more - the fact they're doing this to him with ineffective pain relief, or the fact he's not making a sound.

Two hours later, the infected portion of Gryffin's arm has been removed. The woman had to take more than she initially thought. The infection claimed the majority of his lower arm leaving him with a few inches below his elbow to embed the new connectors to. After the wound heals, the new arm can be fitted and, if his implants are operating as they should, he'll be able to control as he would a flesh arm.

Rayde looks down at the still form on the table.

Once the doctor finished working on him he lost consciousness. His pale chest is rising and falling steadily. No doubt thanks to whatever mechanics or programming he has inside him. 'He good to go?'

The woman nods. 'The arm will do him for a year or so.' She hands Rayde a console. 'This will let you check what's going on inside him. You'll need to hook it to him daily for a few weeks so it can learn what's right and what's wrong with him. I've also added everything you need to increase the arm as needed. I don't want to see you back here again. I don't want any part in whatever is going on with... him.' The way she looks at Gryffin as she says the last word gets Rayde's back up. 'Now pay me and get out of here.'

'My man has the credits.'

The woman gestures to the door. 'After you then. I want to keep my eye on you.'

Rayde smiles as pleasantly as he can while he lifts Gryffin from the table and carries him out of the room. He nods to Creed as he passes. 'We're done here. Kindly pay the woman.'

Rayde brings Gryffin out of the room as the sound of a shot rings out behind him.

ARES

The boy, Gryffin, lifts his head from the floor and watches Rayde step into the room. As always, Rayde sits on the floor and stretches his legs out. 'How are you doing today?'

Gryffin doesn't say anything.

Rayde studies him. Two months have passed since he was brought back to *Ares* and for two months he hasn't uttered a word. He had wondered if the boy was a mute, but from what their less than hi-tech equipment can tell, his vocal cords are undamaged. Everything else had come along better than expected. He was eating solid food. Although still a little unsteady on his feet, he could walk short distances. The wounds from the removal of the implants had healed and the repaired ones seemed to be doing what they should. He still shied away from any physical contact but Rayde wasn't going to argue with him on that. For some reason he also refused to lie on the bed, but he guesses that's more down to habit. Who knows what other quirks he had developed after spending time in that station? It doesn't bear thinking about. So far, despite Ryder's initial concerns, the boy seems to have all his facilities, but perhaps it was still too soon to come to that conclusion.

He moves the plate closer to Gryffin and the boy helps himself to some bread. 'Can you talk at all? I mean, are you able to talk or do you just not fancy it?' He waits a good five minutes but gets nothing back. 'Very well. You eat your dinner. I've got to get back to the command deck. I'll see you later.'

'Can I... come?'

Rayde stops and turns to face Gryffin. The voice is timid and weak, but understandable. He crouches down in front of him again. 'Well, I'll be damned. Nice to know you've got a voice after all. You want to come to the command deck?'

Gryffin nods eagerly. 'Okay then.' He gets up and waits as Gryffin uses the bed to lever himself off the ground. Like a newborn animal, he wobbles for a few seconds, then walks a little unsteadily over to the door.

Rayde adopts a slower pace than usual as he leads Gryffin through the ship. He contacts Creed, telling him to keep the corridors clear and move any non-essential personnel off the command deck while Gryffin is there. He doesn't want to spook him with too many curious stares.

Eventually, they reach the steps leading up to the command platform. Rayde waits at the top as Gryffin crawls on all fours up the stairs then pulls himself upright again. Once he gets to the top, Gryffin stops, hanging on to the railings as he looks around the room. Rayde frowns as he sees the smallest semblance of a smile but dismisses it as a figment of his imagination.

'What do you think?'

Gryffin shuffles over to the railing surrounding the upper platform and looks down at the control stations below him. He points an unsteady finger to the consoles. 'What?'

'What are they?' Gryffin nods. 'They're the controls for the ship. Guidance, navigation, weapons. It's all controlled from here.'

Gryffin turns around and points to the command chair. He opens his mouth but closes it again without saying anything.

'You have to talk, son.' Now that the boy has decided to break his silence, Rayde is going to make sure he keeps talking.

'Yours?'

'That's my command chair. Why don't you try it out?'

Gryffin lowers himself into the chair, appearing so much smaller in the large seat. Rayde turns as Creed clears his throat behind him.

'What is it?'

'A word. In private, sir.'

Rayde nods at Gryffin then joins Creed on the lower level. 'Problem?'

'You're damn right there's a problem. What are you doing, sir?'

'He talked. Asked if he could come here with me.'

'So you took him. To the command deck.'

'I'm not seeing what your problem is.'

'That's the problem, sir. We barely know anything about him. And what we do know is giving me nightmares.' Creed blows out a breath and runs a hand through his dark hair, tucking it behind his ear. 'I understand you want to help him. I get that. Hell, I'm all for that, but it's my job to protect you and this ship. Right now, we know fuck all about him. Don't know who he is. Why he was on the station. What the hell was done to him? How do you know he wasn't planted on that station for us to find. What if we're playing into some unknown hands by giving him full access to the ship.'

'You should rein in that imagination, Creed. He's barely able to walk. I don't see how letting him sit in my chair will come back to bite us. He's not doing any harm.'

'Sir-'

'Enough, Creed. This is my ship. I expect everyone to treat him like a Nomad. That includes you.'

Creed clenches his jaw and nods once. 'Yes, sir.'

'Dismissed.'

Creed takes a deep breath, glances at Gryffin then leaves the command deck. Rayde watches him, an uneasy feeling settling in his gut. He'll have to keep an eye on that one.

ARES

The nightmare starts the same way it always does. Gryffin - or whatever he was called back then - is on the transport with some children he vaguely remembers. They're laughing and joking with each other, then someone comes into the room and tells them to go to sleep.

Then the alarms sound. Then the lights go off. Then the screaming starts.

The nightmares will go one of two ways. He'll either wake up screaming or be thrown into the lab so he can spend some time with the Scientist. Tonight is one of those nights. He's taken by faceless men from the transport with a group of other children and wakes up strapped to the table on the station. He tries to cover his ears as the Scientist hums to himself. He always did that while he worked. The Scientist hovers over him, a wide grin on his face. And then the drill sounds.

Gryffin screams as he comes awake, but he still can't move. He scrambles to free his legs, to get away from wherever he is, panic and terror mixing with the remnants of the dream.

The door opens, filling the small room with light. Gryffin freezes when he sees the large shadow in the doorway. He frantically kicks at whatever has his legs. He needs to get away.

The man steps into the room and crouches down in front of him. 'Hey! It's me. It's Rayde. Calm down. You've got yourself tangled in your covers.'

Gryffin stills as Rayde unwinds the sheet from around his legs and moves it to the side. 'See. You're safe.'

Gryffin nods but he doesn't feel safe. He wants the dreams to stop. He won't be safe until they do.

'You have a nightmare?'

'I was taken and-'

Rayde holds up his hand. 'Shush now. No need to go over the details. Best thing you can do is push it to the back of your mind.'

'Will they stop?'

Rayde nods. 'Up to you though. You're letting the dreams get to you. You fear them so they have this effect on you. You've got to take control of that fear.

Don't let it control you. It's just a dream. Lock the memories away so they can't come out.' He prods Gryffin in the chest. 'Only you can do that.'

Gryffin nods but isn't convinced. 'Why did they sell me?'

'Who?'

'My parents. He said they sold me.'

Rayde sits on the floor beside him and clasps his hands together. 'If that's the case, why are you even asking about them? If they sold you to him knowing what he was going to do, well, that pretty much sums them up. I wouldn't waste another second thinking about them. Won't change a thing, will it.'

Gryffin shakes his head.

'Good. You hungry?'

He shakes his head again. 'Rayde?'

'What?'

'Am I a thing?'

'Are you what?'

Gryffin lifts his metal arm off his knee. 'The woman I got this from. She said I was a thing.'

Rayde sighs loudly and rubs his eyes. 'Listen, I wouldn't be putting much stock in anything she said, daft woman. Ignore her.'

He can't ignore her. What if what she said is true? Rayde didn't say he's not a thing. He's never been treated badly by Rayde or the Nomad, but is that because they're just being kind to him? Do they feel the same way as the woman? He looks down at his arm again and the excitement at having it fades a little. It's not a real arm. That woman just added what the Scientist made for him. She just added what he didn't get a chance to. He knew the Scientist changed him, but did those changes make him more like a machine than a real person?

Rayde gets up and Gryffin recoils when he pats him on the shoulder. 'You've got to stop doing that. I ain't going to hurt you. Forget the dreams, forget your parents and forget that woman.' He taps his forefinger against the side of his head. 'Lock it all away in here. Don't let it control you. You get me?'

Gryffin nods even though he doesn't have the first clue how to do what Rayde is asking him to do.

'Now, I'm going to get you some food. You need to keep your strength up.'

He closes the door behind him, leaving Gryffin on the floor in the dark again. He pulls his knees up to his chest and stares down at his metal arm. He's been trying to forget what the woman had called him, but he can't. He doesn't want to be a thing.

Gryffin climbs to his feet and slowly makes his way down the corridor to the bathroom. He locks the door and looks at himself in the small mirror over the sink. He's still getting used to his reflection. It had been so long since he saw himself it's taking time to accept he's looking at himself. Gryffin lifts his flesh hand and gently touches the implant around his eye. It hurts. He frowns and the skin wrinkles above the implant but the metal doesn't move. It's attached to his... he searches his memory for the word, but he can't find it.

Talking is getting easier, but sometimes he can't remember the words he needs. Like walking, he knows how to do it, but it was so long since he had to do either, he has to concentrate when he's doing it.

He takes the small griffin pendent in his hand. A dark-haired woman gave it to him. He tries to hang on to the memory, tries to pull it out of hiding, but then remembers what Rayde said. Remembering won't help him. He doesn't want to do anything to make Rayde angry. If he was told he couldn't stay on *Ares*, he'd have nowhere to go. No one to protect him in case the Scientist comes looking for him. He lets go of the pendent and tucks it back under his t-shirt. Whoever the woman is, he needs to forget about her. Rayde's right. She must not have been someone who cared about him. If she did, she would have found him before the Scientist hurt him. If anyone cared about him they would have saved him a long time ago. He doesn't want to believe what the Scientist told him, but he must have been telling the truth. No one came for him because no one wanted him.

He wipes away a tear as it trails down his cheek. He hasn't cried for a long time. Crying didn't help any of them in the lab. When they cried the Scientist laughed. Rayde would probably laugh too.

Gryffin sniffs and wipes his face again. He stands tall and takes a deep breath. There's no way he's going to mess this up. If Rayde wants him to not think about what happened, that's what he'll do. He doesn't know how. Even if it means hiding the nightmares from

Rayde and not talking about it.

He lets the woman slip away with all the other fragments of memories. He knows it's the right thing to do but can't help feeling like he's letting someone important go.

PART 3

2 YEARS LATER

GRYFFIN – 17 YEARS OLD
BRAY – 12 YEARS OLD

EARTH

Bray charges his opponent, ramming his shoulder into the other boy's chest. They are swallowed by the crowd briefly before being shoved back in the makeshift ring. Rex is at least five years older than Bray's twelve years but matched in size and ability. Bray loses his footing and lands heavily on Rex. He decides to take advantage and punches him in the nose. Blood splatters over the front of Bray's shirt as the bones in Rex's nose shatter under the impact. Despite his size, the scream that comes out of Rex is high pitched. 'You broke my nose!'

'I'm not finished yet.'

'Oh yes, you are.'

Bray cringes as the crowd scatters, leaving the still shrieking Rex under him. He looks over his shoulder and smiles at the two Foundation security guards. 'Hey, Mace.'

'Brayden Sawyer. Of course it's you. Get up. And it's Officer Alder.'

Without waiting for Bray to comply, Mace hauls him to his feet and shoves him against the wall of the alley. 'What's the damage?'

The other guard helps Rex to his feet and leans over to examine the injury. 'Broken nose.'

'Hurt pride too, am I right?'

Rex wipes his nose on the hem of his shirt as he scowls at Bray.

'Take him home. I'll deal with this one - again.' Bray waves at Rex as he is led away, only stopping when Mace raises his eyebrows at him. 'You just don't know when to quit, do you?'

Bray smiles again and shrugs.

Mace points to his transport. 'Get in.'

'You arresting me?'

'No. I should though. Get in before I change my mind.'

Bray slides into the back seat of the transport and wrinkles his nose. 'Smells strange in here.'

'Just dropped off an interesting character from the outer walls. Personal hygiene wasn't his priority. So, you going to tell me what Rex did or should I guess?'

'Just don't like him.'

'No one does. That doesn't mean you get to pick a fight. I'll do what I can to convince his parents not to take this further, but you can't keep doing this. You'll end up doing something I can't do anything about.'

'He had it coming.'

'Can't disagree. I'm going to take a stab in the dark and guess he said something negative about your brother or your parents. Or maybe it was just that he's around five years older than you. Just like the last time. And the time before that. You must know we see what you're doing. You can't take out your anger at your brother on these idiots just because they're in the same age group.'

Bray looks down, frowning at a wet patch on the floor. A present left by the man Mace had arrested before him. Mace was wrong about the age thing. It's just a coincidence everyone that pisses him off is around the same age Daegan would be if he had stayed on Earth with his family instead of leaving. He hit Rex because he said Bray's parents didn't want him. That's why they had sent him to live with Morgan and Shayla. Bray knows he lives on Earth because his parents want him to have a good life, but hearing that from Rex had pissed him off. He didn't need that from a rich, spoilt brat like Rex. So what if his mother wasn't married when she had Daegan. So what if his parents have to hide from the Foundation while on Earth because she wouldn't be legally allowed back. So what if they spent too much time looking for Daegan and not enough with him. So what if they disappeared two years ago just like Daegan did. So what if – just like with Daegan – the search parties had been called back when it was decided they weren't going to find anything.

'You got to toughen up, Bray,' Mace says, looking over his shoulder at him. 'Brats like Rex will always have something to say. His words have to mean nothing to you, otherwise he'll keep winning by winding you up. And then you'll be back here again.'

Mace holds up his hand to silence Bray as a call comes in through his earpiece. He listens in silence, his posture stiffening. He's just got bad news. Maybe he won't be able to bring him home. He might get dropped off here and that suits him fine. At least he'd have a few hours before Morgan got the news about what happened.

Mace finishes the call and is silent for another few minutes. When he speaks again, it's random chit-chat. There's something on his mind but Bray doesn't want to know what it is. He'll have enough problems of his own when Morgan hears about what happened with Rex.

Fifteen minutes later, Mace brings the transport down in front of the farmhouse and shuts off the engine. 'Wait here a minute.'

Bray shrinks down in the seat as the front door opens and Morgan appears. Great. There go his few hours of peace. Morgan and Shayla are going to kill him. Mace and Morgan speak for a few minutes. Mace Alder has taken Bray home too many times to count. Bray can't stand the Foundation or the guards, but

Mace is decent. He graduated a few years ago so must be in his mid-twenties and is nothing like any of the Foundation guards Bray's met. Mace's parents lived under the radar like his did. Someone with connections had fixed his records so he appeared a legitimate candidate. With enough credits, anything could be fixed. Mace did what he could to help Bray, smoothing things over when he took things a little too far. He can't help it if people push him. They were asking for trouble so he gave it to them. He'd heard the same sermon from Morgan and Mace. Rise above it. Don't let it get to you. It's just words. Blah, blah, blah. Doing nothing won't stop the people talking. Making them stop - that was the only way.

Mace and Morgan walk towards the transport. Bray prepares his speech. He wanted to make sure he got his side across straight away.

Morgan opens the door of the transport and Bray steps out. 'I know-'

'Bray, Maggie and Dean...' Morgan curses and shakes his head.

Bray looks from Morgan to Mace and knows something is seriously wrong. 'They found Mum and Dad? Morgan?'

Morgan sniffs and takes a deep breath. 'Bray, they found their transport. It crashed on a sparsely habited colony shortly after they left Earth. They didn't... they're dead. I'm so sorry, son.' Morgan places his hand on Bray's shoulder but Bray takes a step back shaking his head.

'No way! This isn't funny, Morgan. Stop it!'

'I wish I could. I can't tell you how much I wish this wasn't happening, but it is.'

'Where? Where did they crash?'

'Danath. One of the border colonies.'

'They wouldn't crash. Dad's the best pilot I know. He wouldn't crash. It's a mistake.'

Mace steps closer and Bray points his finger at him. 'Don't!' Mace steps back and shoves his hands into his back pockets. 'Why are you still here? Go!'

'Don't be having a go at Mace. This isn't his fault.'

'Yeah, well someone made a mistake because it's not them, okay!'

'There was a DNA test done. It matched.'

'So where are they then?'

'Bray, the transport was destroyed. There's nothing left. I'm so sorry.'

Bray stares at his uncle then spots Shayla and Erin in the doorway. Tears are running down Shayla's face and Erin is hugging her mother. Bray shakes his head as he takes a few steps back. He can't be here with them. Not if they're going to believe this pack of lies someone is giving them. Before Mace can stop him, he pushes past and runs away from them and the lies.

∞

Bray hides his face as someone lowers onto the ground beside him. The scent of Shayla's perfume is like a comforting blanket wrapping itself around him.

But he doesn't want her comfort. What he wants is his family back. He'd hung on to the denial as long as he could but eventually it turned to tears and now he can't stop them.

It's not fair. Why did he have to lose his brother and now his parents? Is this punishment for getting in trouble? If he had behaved, if he'd gone to school every day and didn't argue with Morgan so much would he still have a family?

He sniffs and clenches his jaw. No, this isn't his fault. This is Daegan's fault. If Daegan hadn't been a selfish ass his parents would still be alive. His brother had messed everything up.

Shayla doesn't say or do anything, just keeps him company as he cries. He doesn't know how long it takes for him to get control of himself again. He sniffs and wipes his nose on his sleeve. Shayla hands him a tissue which he accepts with another sniff.

'Are they sure it's them?'

'They're sure, Bray.'

It was a stupid thing to ask, but a part of him wanted to hang on to hope. 'What happens now?'

'What do you mean?'

'What happens to me?'

Shayla shuffles around to sit opposite him. She takes his hand, holding on when he tries to pull away from her touch. 'This is your home, Bray. That will never change. You're as much a part of our family as Erin is. We love you so much, Bray.'

'But I keep messing up. I make you guys so angry.

Why would you want me to stay?'

She smiles and tucks a stray lock of hair behind his ear. 'Perhaps you could ease off on that a little. Or we're going to have to offer Mace room and board since he spends so much time here. Morgan just gets angry because he can see how much potential you have. Acting up, fighting, all that lashing out, it's not going to do you any good in the long run. We both get frustrated when you waste that potential. That doesn't mean we're going to turn our backs on you though.'

'I'll try to be better.'

'I know things haven't been easy for you and losing Maggie and Dean...' she pauses and looks away for a minute. 'Losing them like this... it's not fair. Especially after what happened to Daegan. I wish I could take the pain from you. I wish there were some words I could say that would help, but there isn't.'

'I'm an orphan now, right?'

She wraps her arms around him and holds him as he cries again. 'No, Bray. You're our son.'

PART 4

3 YEARS LATER

GRYFFIN – 20 YEARS OLD
BRAY – 15 YEARS OLD

ARES

Gryffin lowers onto the bed and stares over at the holster on the floor against the far wall. It was a gift from Rayde. The captain has the gun in his room. He said he'd look after it until Gryffin needed it. Gryffin didn't mind. Being trusted to have his own gun is something he never thought would happen. Rayde had been training him every day when he wasn't needed on the command deck. He was getting stronger, faster, and was able to keep up with some of the newer Nomad while sparring.

Rayde had let him leave the ship today with one of the raiding parties. For the first time since being rescued, he felt like he finally belonged to something. The other Nomad kept away from him, but he's used to that. He hadn't spent much time with them over the last few years. Rayde trained him, Rayde ate with him, and Rayde checked his implants.

Maybe after Rayde's announcement today, he'll finally be accepted. Rayde had made him a Nomad. No rank but part of the group like everyone else on the ship. Rayde didn't assign him to an area, but said he could spend some time in engineering when he wasn't training. If he can keep getting better, keep training maybe he can get assigned to the command deck. He'd only been there once after he first arrived, but he'll never forget it.

He smiles as he closes his eyes, trying to remember every detail of the deck, until someone knocks on his door.

Fully expecting Rayde, he takes a step back when he finds two Nomad at his door.

'Rayde wants you in the training room. C'mon.'

Gryffin hesitates. He doesn't know these men. 'Where's Rayde?'

'Waiting for you. Move or we'll all get in shit with him.'

Gryffin nods and doesn't say anything else. He follows the men through the ship, ducking through a hatch, careful not to hit his head. Being taller than most of the Nomad on the ship means he spends most his time stooped over to get through the cramped corridors of the bottom decks.

The lead Nomad opens the door to the training room and he is pushed inside, the door sealing behind him. Gryffin freezes when he sees the walkway filled with Nomad. He scans the faces but can't see Rayde or Creed.

'What's going on?'

The only response he gets is to be forcefully shoved down the stairs and into the centre of the room as the crowd shouts at him. He can't make out everything they're saying, but he hears the word 'freak' quite a lot. He swallows deeply and crosses his arm over his chest. After a lot of effort, he finally gets his metal arm to follow the other across his chest. Rayde added parts to his arm yesterday to make it fit him better, but he's not used to the extra weight yet.

He turns in a circle trying to find some way out, but as he turns, more Nomad step into the room. Rayde has only taught him to count to twelve. The gun he's allowed to train with holds twelve rounds. Rayde said learning any more numbers would be a waste of time. Looking around the room there's a lot more than twelve men facing him. Maybe even the whole crew.

'What's going on?' he asks again.

'Rayde thinks you have what it takes to be a Nomad.' A tall, broad Nomad called Kellyn steps forward. He's trained with him a few times. Kellyn doesn't like him. The Nomad crosses his well-muscled, heavily tattooed arms. 'The problem we have is that he's skipped the deal-breaker part of the training.' The man gestures to his friends. 'Each of us - every man here had to fight for their place on the crew.' He waves a dismissive hand at Gryffin. 'All except you. You don't think that's fair, do you?'

Gryffin doesn't answer. He doesn't know what to say.

'So, we've decided to rectify that. You're going to fight all of us. If you win, we'll let you be a Nomad.'

'But Rayde said I'm a Nomad.'

The harsh laugh reminds Gryffin of the Scientist. An involuntary shiver runs down his spine. 'This is between you and us. No need to get the captain involved.'

Without another word Gryffin finds himself being approached by all the men at once. The screaming, chanting and shouting soars to a painful level. He covers his ears against the onslaught of noise but it just makes everyone shout even louder.

The first blow from behind sends him sprawling onto his front. He quickly rolls over just in time to shield his face from a large fist heading its way. He drops his arms as a kick meets with his ribs and another with his legs. Gryffin curls into a tight ball and tries to block out the attack but there are too many of them. He detaches from the pain, just like he did every time the Scientist touched him. He feels the blows hitting him, breaking bones and bruising skin, but he's powerless to stop them.

This wasn't supposed to happen anymore. Rayde said no one would hurt him again. Rayde said he would make him strong and able to fight for himself.

So what is he doing curled up in a ball on the floor? Maybe this is a test from Rayde? Maybe if he fails, Rayde will kick him off the ship? Maybe he'll bring him back to the station?

Out of nowhere, the urge to fight, to survive, overpowers everything else he's feeling. A stab of pain tears through his head, forcing a scream out. The sound of his pain adds fuels to the attack which grows in ferocity.

Like a blade slicing into his head, the pain travels up the side of Gryffin's scalp and stops at his eyes. His stomach lurches as his vision swims and clears. If he wasn't being attacked he would have taken some time to enjoy being able to see properly.

A rib cracks, driving the air from his lungs. A quiet calm settles on him. He's aware of the blows, feels the impact but doesn't feel the pain. The helplessness he felt while with the Scientist morphs into something else, something much stronger.

Anger.

He never felt angry before. Scared but never angry. Until now. These men are trying to ruin things for him. They're trying to make him scared again. Trying to break him again.

He feels a slight tingle in his metal arm, building to a searing pain along the whole prosthetic. At the same time, the blows are replaced by shouts and screams from his attackers.

Gryffin opens his eyes, gasping when he sees what looks like electricity coursing down his mechanical arm, gathering around his fist. Instead of wondering what's going on, he focuses on the first Nomad he sees.

He swings at the man's legs and connects with his knee. The blow surprises both of them. The man screams as his leg crumples from under him. Gryffin dismisses him as he pushes to his feet. He targets another man, somehow firing electricity from his metal arm, hitting him in the chest.

Realising the tables have turned, the Nomad try to escape, but it's too late for that. A strange calm takes over. The men surrounding him aren't Nomad anymore. They're targets. He tries to back away from them but he's not in control of what's happening. Rayde's training is mixing with something else deep inside him. Something he hasn't felt before.

Movement behind him triggers that unfamiliar part of himself. There's no rhyme or reason to his attack. The anger is a living being inside him, lashing out at anyone close enough. His fist connects with someone's face, followed by a sweeping kick to someone's chest. Every strike hits home. If the target is too far away, a shot of electricity from his arm takes care of them. All around him, Nomad are falling.

After the men on the training floor are dealt with, Gryffin looks up at the targets frozen in place on the balcony above him. He leaps up, grabbing onto the railing running along the viewing level. With a strength he didn't know he had, he swings his legs up, landing on the platform in front of the crowd.

He pauses as Rayde steps forward, his hands raised

in front of him. Gryffin knows he should stop fighting, but he can't. He doesn't know how to. Instead, he lashes out, catching Creed as he steps in between Gryffin and the captain. Before he can turn around, Gryffin is tackled from behind. He is forced onto his front, the cold metal walkway digging painfully into the side of his face. He tries to get up but it feels like he has half the crew on his back.

Searing pain shoots through the side of his face, along the implant and everything goes quiet.

ARES

Rayde stands up as Creed steps into the holding cell. He's been sitting with Gryffin for the last three hours. The young man lost consciousness after he screamed in pain and hasn't stirred since. Ryder still hasn't made it down to see to his many wounds. Blood is smeared over his face and hair, a few fingers are broken, and his arm is shattered. That's just what Rayde can see. He'll have to wait for treatment until Ryder is free.

Creed passes Rayde a drink and crosses his arms. 'Anything yet?'

Rayde takes a sip then shakes his head. 'Nothing.

Did you find out what the hell the crew was playing at?'

'Nomad rules state every new crew member has to fight for their place.'

'And I decided to let Gryffin on the crew without that. My decision. My ship and my fucking rules! What the hell were they doing? We're on the same side, Creed. He's one of us.'

'Yes, but the men don't agree. A lot of them don't trust him. Don't trust what he is. Hell, don't know what he is. They feel it should be the same rules for everyone, sir.'

'Yeah, and what are they saying about that now?'

Creed winces. 'Kellyn may never say anything again. It's even odds on him waking up at all. Twenty-three injured. That's more than half the crew.'

Rayde rubs a hand over his jaw and sighs. 'Damn it. Stupid fools.'

'If it's any consolation, I doubt anyone will be taking him on again. Any idea what the hell he did with his arm?'

'No clue. I need to talk to him whenever he wakes up. If he wakes up. Find out what exactly he did.'

'Would any of the modifications we made have done that?'

Rayde shakes his head. 'Doubt it. The inner bones of the limb, if you want to call them that, are the original parts he was found with. We've just added to the outer layers as he's grown. We still don't have the first clue what half of the metal does. As for this electricity trick, that's certainly a new one.'

'Trick? He could have killed the lot of us!'

'But he didn't.'

'Only because he blacked out. He was aiming for your head. That action alone is enough to justify putting a bullet in his.'

'We're not killing him.'

'He threatened the life of the captain.'

'He didn't recognise me.'

'How is that an argument for keeping him alive?' Creed lowers onto the ground and leans against the door frame. 'I get why you want to give him a second chance. But this is playing with fire, sir. He's dangerous. Sir, do you not think it would be better to... relocate him?'

'To where exactly? We can't just drop him off at the nearest colony and walk away. No, we've come too far with him. He's making real improvements.'

'Improvements? Sir, there's a 50/50 chance he's killed one of the crew and was on his way to killing you. It took twelve of us to hold him down. He's barely got any meat on his bones. He shouldn't have been able to overpower a dozen highly trained Nomad.'

'It wasn't him.'

'It looked like him to me.'

Rayde shakes his head. 'That's not what I mean. Did you see his eyes - especially the one with the metal around it? There was a purple glow in it.'

'What are you saying, sir? That he's possessed or something like that?'

'Of course that's not what I'm saying. There is a hell

of a lot about the lad we don't understand. One thing is sure - he was modified for a reason. Perhaps this is it.'

'What? Beating on the crew?'

'Fighting.'

Rayde turns to look at Creed but the man isn't on the same track as him. 'Think about it. As you said, it took a lot to restrain him. Whatever was done to him has made him stronger. Why would that be needed?'

Creed makes a face then shrugs. 'I guess you have a point. But that just proves mine. He needs to go.'

'I'll make that decision. Dismissed.'

Rayde walks around the cell as Creed climbs the steps to the upper level. Creed may not see the potential in Gryffin, but Rayde does. He's proud of the Nomad, but the group isn't quite where he would like them to be. If they're to have any chance at a long and profitable future, something needs to change. He looks at the skeleton of a boy lying broken and bleeding on the floor of the cell. If he can somehow harness whatever is inside him, use it to build a solid future for the Nomad, it's worth the work. It's worth the risk.

11

ARES

Gryffin squeezes his eyes shut and groans. Every muscle, every bone, every nerve in his body is on fire. The creaks and groans of *Ares* echo loudly in his head, the sounds bouncing around his skull like a spiked metal ball. He wants to cover his ears but his body isn't doing what he wants.

Something cool is placed on his forehead, helping to ease the band of pain squeezing the top of his skull like a vice.

'You with me, son?'

He doubts Rayde shouted at him but that's what it sounds like. Gryffin grunts in response and gags as his stomach ejects the small amount he ate for breakfast. A heavy weight rests on his back, gripping his shoulder. Deep down he knows it's Rayde's hand, but the feel of it is more than he can bear. His metal hand is dead so he uses his heavy legs to push him along the ground, removing Rayde's hand from him.

'Sorry, son. Just trying to help. Can you open your eyes?'

He doesn't bother trying. Getting his stomach to obey is the priority. Feeling slowly returns to his fingers then his hands, but he still can't move them. He's restrained. Panic quickly replaces the confusion, bringing his brain back into this world with a bang. He struggles to break free, but the heavy chains won't budge.

'Relax, son. Just don't want you hurting yourself. Take it easy. I'll let you out soon.'

He does as he's told. He doesn't have a choice. Ignoring the restraints, he tries to calm down, letting his body recover from whatever's wrong with it. As feeling returns, the pain in his head is met with more pain from his body. His real arm is in agony. Every breath is a struggle and sends shards of pain through his chest. He licks his dry lips, tasting blood. 'What... happened?'

He hears rustling and Rayde's voice comes from near his head. 'I was kinda hoping you could shed some light on that. You put twenty-three Nomad in the med bay.'

His eyes finally obey and he squints up at Rayde.

His captain is crouched on the ground beside him. He looks over Rayde's shoulder and frowns when he notices the heavy bars of the detention cell. 'I don't...' Why can't he remember what happened? 'My arm...'

'Why don't I tell you what I know? The crew, well most of the crew, ambushed you. Against my orders, I'll add. They beat the living crap out of you. Broke your arm, two of your fingers, three ribs and bruised you good. Ryder checked you out. You'll hurt like hell for a bit but you'll recover. Your arm is supported in a pressure bandage but I'm not too eager to remove the restraints. Sorry if that's not helping the pain, but I need to understand what happened. The bit that's confusing the hell out of us is what you did. One minute they were kicking the shit out of you, which I will deal with, believe me. Then you get electricity running down your arm and you retaliate. In less than ten seconds you had taken down most of the crew. Nearly got me too, but you blacked out.'

Gryffin hears everything Rayde is saying but it won't sink into his head.

'Well?'

'I don't remember.'

Rayde sighs. 'I was afraid you'd say that.'

Gryffin rolls onto his side to ease pressure from his ribs but that just puts more pressure on his broken arm. He's exhausted and sore. All he wants to do is sleep.

Rayde carefully lays a blanket over him. 'We'll talk when you're with it a little more. I'll leave you on the floor. Don't want to move you. You're beaten up enough.'

'Do I have to leave *Ares*?'

Rayde pauses. 'No. We do need to figure out what happened though. Get some rest and we'll talk when you're healed. You don't have to worry about the crew. No one will touch you again. Understood?'

Gryffin nods then allows his body the sleep it desperately needs.

12

Gryffin bites the inside of his mouth as Rayde's sparring stick breaks the skin on his bare back. 'You can stop this, son. Just use it.'

Gryffin gasps in pain as the metal rod meets his flesh again. 'I'm trying.'

'Try harder!' Gryffin clenches his fist as Rayde strikes him again. He knows Rayde is just trying to make him stronger, but using the implant to stop the pain isn't top on his list. After what happened a few days ago, he hates the damn thing. He grits his teeth as the room spins. Rayde shoves him from behind with the tip of his stick. Gryffin snarls and pulls against the chains securing his ankle to the floor. 'Stop.'

Rayde laughs at him and pokes him again. 'Make me.'

Gryffin closes his eyes and tries to bring back the feelings that triggered the control implant, but he can't. When it took over before, he didn't consciously do anything. One minute he was being attacked by the crew, and the next he was in a cell. He doesn't remember what happened during the missing time. If he's being honest, he doesn't want to remember. The pain after he came to was nearly as bad as some of the procedures he went through.

'C'mon, son. Give in to it.'

Gryffin shakes his head. 'Please, sir. I don't want-'

Rayde's weapon strikes him again, knocking his still-healing arm. 'Don't beg. Nomads don't beg.'

'I don't want this.'

Rayde shoves him back harder. Gryffin trips over the chain securing him to the floor and lands in a heap. Rayde leans over, pushing him to the floor with the end of his stick. 'You'd prefer to go back to the station? You attacked my crew, son. Unless you can pull your weight, prove you have a place on the ship, I'm going to be in an awkward position. Give me something to work with at least. If you can take down a room full of Nomad without breaking a sweat, you're going to be invaluable. But only if you can control it. You're no good to us if you can't bring it out and control it. You understand that right? I can't have you attacking the crew whenever one of them looks at you the wrong way.'

Gryffin's heart races at the mention of the station. The years that passed since he was saved disappear. He's thrown back into the lab, back into the pain, back into the dark, into the cold. He squeezes his eyes shut as the memories attack him, bringing the pain to life again. A ball of pressure builds at the base of his skull, but he loses the connection with it. It disappears back to where it came from.

'What happened the last time? How did you let it out?'

'I don't know! They were hurting me and it just happened. I didn't do anything.'

Rayde looks down at his hand, resting on the hilt of the blade he always carries on his belt. He looks back at Gryffin again. 'You trust me, son?'

Gryffin doesn't like the way Rayde's hand is tightening around the blade. 'I don't know how to do it again.'

'I hear you. Get up. Move towards me, as far as the chain will let you.' Once Gryffin has extended his bonds as much as he can Rayde pulls the blade out of its holster. 'Lift your arms over your head.'

Gryffin hesitates not liking where this is heading.

'Do it!'

When he does as ordered, Rayde slices the blade across his exposed side, releasing a stream of blood. Rayde turns the knife around and pushes the hilt against the wound. The jolt of pain does the trick. The pressure rises, moving from the base of his skull around the side of his head. His vision sharpens and he sucks in a breath as a piercing pain embeds itself around his ocular implant. He focuses on Rayde and barely manages to hold himself back as his mentor smiles. 'That's good, son. Let it take control.' Rayde activates a training drone and steps aside as the large machine makes its way over to Gryffin.

Gryffin rolls to the side as the machine takes a shot at his head, driving its foot into the floor. He jumps to his feet and slams his boot into the drone's side, followed by his fist to the side of its face. The machine retaliates but it is no match for Gryffin. Gryffin feels like a passenger in his own body as something else takes control of his actions. He tries to pull control back but whatever Rayde wanted him to set free won't let him have a say in what happens. Before the machine can turn around, Gryffin cocks his arm and rams his fist into the base of the drone's neck, severing the head from the rest of the body. The drone slumps to the ground, sparks springing from the remains of its torso.

With nothing else to occupy whatever has control of him, Gryffin turns to face Rayde. The Nomad already has a heavy-duty stun gun pointed at his chest. 'Pull it back, son. Control it.'

Trapped inside his head, Gryffin wants to laugh. Easier said than done - especially when it wants nothing more than to keep going. He takes a step towards Rayde, but the chain stops him.

Rayde takes a step back, the stun gun pointed at

Gryffin's chest. 'You're doing good. Control it.'

The training room door slides open and a man is shoved down the stairs. Gryffin watches in confusion as Rayde drags the man to his feet and holds him up in front of Gryffin. 'This man was part of the team that stood up to us on the last raid. He's my prisoner. Not worth anything to us alive. Dead, however... he can send a message about us. You don't stand in the way of the Nomad. How about you send that message.'

Lost to the implant, he hears the words but can't do a thing about what his body is doing. He stares down at the man, seeing the fear in his face.

'You've been training every day since I found you,' Rayde continues. 'You've proved you're capable of being a Nomad, but now it's time to show me you have what it takes to lead a team. You need to prove you have the guts to do whatever you need to get your team home in one piece.'

The man silently stares at Gryffin, still chained to the floor like some crazed animal.

'Show me you have what it takes. Show me I didn't make a mistake all those years ago.' Gryffin doesn't move. Nothing to do with him, the implant in his head doesn't see the man as a threat. Or maybe it's not used to being told what to do. Rayde throws a knife in front of the prisoner. 'He's an armed threat, Gryffin. Take him down.'

The man may be many things but a threat isn't one of them. Killing for the good of the group is one thing. Murdering someone like this... it's not something he wants to do. He doesn't know how, but he manages to keep his body in place. He looks up at Rayde and knows he's running out of time. The impatience is beginning to show in the older man's face. He pulls the blade out of its scabbard and spins it in his hand. The unspoken threat is all the convincing Gryffin needs.

Rayde smiles and speaks to the man. 'Pick up that knife. Might as well go out fighting.' The man does as he's told. He tests the blade in his hands and smiles slightly when he realises the person facing him is chained to the floor.

He lunges at Gryffin, sensing the small possibility of coming out of this alive. Gryffin reacts, no more in control of what he's doing then the man is to stop it.

Gryffin lunges at the man driving him to the ground. Gryffin's knee presses against the man's chest as he twists the hand holding the knife. The man's wrist breaks and the knife falls to the ground. Gryffin reaches for it, but Rayde stops him.

'You don't need that. Use your hands.'

The man tears at Gryffin's leg, trying to get free. He bucks under him, but Gryffin holds his position. He slams his metal fist into the man's face, dislodging a few teeth.

'That's it. Keep going.'

Rayde's encouragement continues until the man stills under him. With the target taken care of Gryffin turns to face Rayde, but the Nomad is prepared for him. A few hits from the stun gun send him slumping back on the ground beside the man he just killed.

When he wakes, he's in the cell again lying on the floor.

'Welcome back, son. You've only been out for an hour. Improvement on the last time.'

Gryffin stares in horror at the dried blood on his hand. He tries to wipe it off on his trouser leg but it won't budge.

'C'mon. Let's get you back to your room.' Rayde offers him a hand and pulls him to his feet. He slaps him on the back, showering him with praise, but the words don't register with Gryffin. The floor tilts under his feet and Rayde swims dizzily from side to side. 'You good?'

Gryffin shakes his head and doubles over as his stomach cramps.

'Calm yourself. You went like this the last time you did that trick of yours. Must be some sort of reset within the components.'

Gryffin nods once, desperately trying to get control of his body. He can't remember feeling this horrible. His body isn't sore - it just feels wrong. Like his skin doesn't fit him. The metal parts feel like they're overheating and the flesh surrounding them throbs angrily. Every breath threatens to bring the contents of his stomach up and he's half expecting the top of his head to pop off with the building pressure in his skull. He wants nothing more than to crawl into his bed and stay there.

Rayde continues talking to him but the words don't make sense. Not seeming to notice, Rayde takes

Gryffin's arm, supporting him as they make their way through the ship. All his concentration goes into putting one foot in front of the other until they finally reach his room.

'You okay?'

Gryffin nods again and manages to make it into his room without tripping over his own feet. 'You want me to stay?'

Gryffin shakes his head once, wincing as the metal ball thumps against the inside of his skull.

'I'll check on you in a bit. You did real good, son.'

Rayde slaps him on the shoulder and walks away, disappearing around the corner. Once the door closes Gryffin stumbles towards the bed, tripping over his feet and hitting his head against the small table beside his bed. He touches his forehead and his fingers come away covered in blood. With everything else going on with his body a cut is a minor problem. Cradling his still healing arm to his chest he drags himself over to his bed but loses the battle with his stomach. He changes direction, aiming for the container in the corner of the room. His stomach decides not to wait that long. He groans and moves away from the mess back towards his low cot and pulls himself up. He collapses on the thin cover and squeezes his eyes shut. The room spins, so he grabs on to the sides of the bed to stop himself falling off.

Dark patches form at the edge of his vision and creep in, turning his room black. He reaches out for his comms unit but gropes blindly as his eyes shut down.

Before he can completely freak out, spasms of pain work through his implant. His back arches and he digs his fingers into the bed as he holds back a scream. He closes his eyes and clenches his metal fist. Sparks of electricity jump over his arm, sending more ripples of pain through his body. If he could, he'd happily tear the thing from his body and throw it out the nearest airlock. The weight of the new arm is excruciating on the sensitive connectors embedded in his stump.

Gryffin runs his hand along his metal arm, stopping at the join where his flesh locks into the limb. He was told to leave his arm on, but he can't think past the pain. He feels along the joint trying to locate the two connectors under the arm. It takes longer than he wants thanks to his twisted stomach and dud eyes, but he eventually finds the connectors, pushes them in and turns his upper arm to unlock it from the prosthetic. Biting back a scream he pulls his arm free and drops the metal part on the floor. Gryffin falls back on his bed, cradling his damaged arms against his chest, trying not to put any pressure on the cut on his side Rayde gave him. The swaying sensation ramps up a gear so he gives up on the bed. The landing is far from smooth, but at least he can't fall off the floor. Shame and disgust push past the no emotion wall Rayde was helping him build.

Stuck on his front on the cold metal floor, Gryffin closes his eyes. His broken arm is pressed under his chest but without his prosthetic attached, he can't lever himself up. He tries to tell himself the tears running down his face are from pain, but he's not convinced. He's pathetic. He doubts Creed would be crying on the floor after killing someone. If he can't get a grip of himself, Rayde won't be able to keep him on board. Then what would happen to him? Where would he go? It's not like anyone else would take him in. The Nomad gave him back his life and he's repaying them by crying on the floor. No wonder the rest of the crew attacked him when Rayde allowed him into the group. He hasn't proved himself.

The pressure around the top of his head increases. He tastes blood in his mouth and realises he bit his tongue to stop himself screaming.

He's not going to let Rayde and the Nomad down. The only way to prove himself is to do exactly what Rayde wants him to do. He'll fight to be the best Nomad he can be. He'll do anything to stay on the crew and repay his debt to Rayde. The invisible hand twists his gut. There's time for that when this pain ends. He allows the tears out as he curls into a ball and rocks himself to a nightmare-filled sleep.

13

Creed pauses at the door, his hand hovering above the control panel. He didn't plan on coming here, but in the eight hours since the incident in the training room, he's been unable to get the replay out of his head. He had watched the whole fight - well, the slaughter from the balcony.

He'd seen some messed up stuff in his life, but that was on a new level. He's not bothered by the death of the man, it's the way he was killed that's keeping the images in his head. It was like dangling a rabbit in front of a hungry dog. Gryffin would have killed the guy - no question, but not like that. It was a game to

Rayde. It was like he was trying to see how far he could push Gryffin before he'd snap. And that's what's worrying Creed - the snap.

By taking that life, Rayde had forced Gryffin along a path he didn't need to take. Being a Nomad is about more than killing. Gryffin could have been part of the crew without becoming a murderer. He takes a deep breath and presses his hand to the panel. The door slides aside revealing Gryffin, sitting on the floor alone, in the dark. His knees are pulled up to his chest and he's staring ahead at nothing in particular. The newly adjusted metal arm is on the ground beside him. Rayde wouldn't be happy about that. Fuck him.

Creed guesses he's maybe a decade or so older than Gryffin, but sometimes when he looked at him, it was like he was looking at a child. Like right now. 'You okay?'

Gryffin nods, but he doesn't take his eyes off the blood on his fist. Creed curses Rayde. He made Gryffin kill then put him back in his room without letting him clean the other man's blood off him. Even in the gloom, he can see the shakes working through the younger man's body. He's in shock. 'C'mon.'

Gryffin tears his eyes from the blood and looks up at Creed.

'You need to get cleaned up and get some food.' Gryffin gets to his feet but struggles to walk without help. 'The aftereffects gone?'

'Nearly. Just tired.'

Gryffin leans heavily on the sink, the short walk

taking whatever energy reserves he had left. Creed washes the blood off Gryffin's hand and arm then helps him back into his room. He pulls a clean t-shirt out of the cubby hole and drops it on the cot next to a fresh pair of trousers. 'Get changed. I'll be back in a few minutes.'

Creed fills a tray with some rations in the mess and heads back to Gryffin's room. When he gets back Gryffin is changed and sitting on the floor again. Creed sits on the edge of the bed and places the plate of food on the floor. 'My first kill was during a raid. Someone tried to kill me. Just lucky I got there first. You've got to move on from it. It'll drive you insane if you don't.'

'You were defending yourself.'

Creed nods. 'Yeah. Different to what happened today, I know.'

'He said the man was trying to hurt him.'

Creed nods. The man was no more a threat to Rayde than Creed himself was. Which right now didn't mean as much as it should. 'I know. You did what you had to do. All you can do now is move on. It won't be the last life you take. Being a Nomad isn't easy. We always seem to be fighting someone.' He laughs and rests his arms on his legs. 'Not saying you'll get used to it, but you'll learn to deal with it. You're a hell of a fighter, Gryffin - with or without whatever's in your head. If you can hone that part, maybe you won't have to depend on letting it control you. I'll bet you could do without the pain after.'

Gryffin nods tiredly. 'I don't want to go back to the

lab.'

'The lab is gone. We destroyed it. Whatever happens, you're never going back there.'

'It's gone?'

'Yeah? Thought Rayde would have told you that?' Creed has the horrible feeling he might have just put his foot in it, but can't think how. 'Best keep it to yourself then. So, you still more comfortable on the floor?'

Gryffin looks up at the bed. 'It feels strange.'

'Yeah, I guess it would. How long were you in that place for? Do you remember?'

'Rayde said not to talk about it.'

Creed clenches his jaw. Figures Rayde would do that. Anything to keep Gryffin isolated from everyone else. Keep him locked in his memories with no way of letting them out or dealing with them except on his terms. 'I'm heading to the mess for some grub. You coming?'

'You gave me food.'

'Thought you could do with getting out of here for a while.'

Gryffin shakes his head. 'Rayde wants me to stay here.'

Creed gestures to the plate. 'Pass me some of the white stuff. Think it's supposed to be bread of some sort.' Gryffin does as he's told, as usual, and Creed takes a bite. He doesn't want to be here in this depressing room with Gryffin but he can't leave him alone after what Rayde made him do. It'll just drive him further into his head, and that's not a good place for anyone.

PART 5

1 YEAR LATER

GRYFFIN – 21 YEARS OLD
BRAY – 16 YEARS OLD

14

'You really don't have to give me a lift home. I can walk.'

The Foundation officer ignores Bray's comment as he concentrates on the controls. The security transport dips as he makes a turn, taking them back out of the city. Bray settles into the seat and gazes out the window. He's going to be grounded for a few years once he gets home, he might as well enjoy his last few minutes of freedom.

The transport lights pick up the large farmhouse as they approach. A lone figure is standing in the open doorway, his tall frame elongated in shadow. Bray can't stop the groan that escapes. Morgan is going to kill him.

The transport lands and Bray is dragged out of the back. Morgan's only acknowledgement is to point to the open doorway. Bray silently obeys, leaving his uncle and the officer to talk.

Bray shuffles into the kitchen and slumps down at the table. Shayla is at the other end, her hands wrapped around a cup of coffee. She continues to stare into the murky liquid as Morgan finishes up outside.

After five minutes of unbearable silence, Morgan slams the front door and storms into the kitchen. He leans back against the work surface, his arms firmly crossed over his chest.

Bray opens his mouth to speak but is silenced when Morgan holds up a finger. 'You don't talk until I'm done.'

Bray sighs dramatically and closes his mouth.

Morgan slams his hand down on the table, making Bray jump in surprise. 'This some sort of joke?'

'No—'

'Stop acting like it is then. This is your life, Brayden. It's serious.'

'It's not a big deal.'

Morgan's mouth drops open. 'Excuse me! Not a big deal? Three of the guys you were with have been arrested for selling guns. It's a bloody miracle you're sitting here and not on your way to a prison moon. Boy, I'm no idiot. I know full well you were as involved as the others were. It's blind luck that you weren't caught with your hands physically on anything. You're sixteen-years-old. It would have been life for you.' Morgan wipes his hands over his face and blows out a long breath. 'Guns? What the hell were you thinking, Bray? Please enlighten us.'

Bray shrugs. 'I don't know what you're complaining about. You said you wanted me to find something I was good at.'

Morgan clenches his jaw and takes a step towards Bray, but Shayla holds up her hand to stop him. 'Losing your temper won't help, Morgan.' He curses and turns away to calm down. Shayla lowers her hand and looks across the table at him. 'Why are you so determined to throw your life away? Are you that unhappy living with us?'

Bray inwardly grimaces. Shayla always knows how to make him feel guilty. 'It's got nothing to do with you and I'm not throwing my life away. You're just upset I'm not following after Erin.'

'That's unfair, Bray,' Shayla responds. 'We've never pushed you to follow Erin — not once. We know you're different and have chosen different paths, but this isn't the right path for you. Surely you must see that? You are so bright. You can make a difference without making a choice that will end with you locked up.'

'How? How can I make a difference behind a desk in the council building? I don't want to do what the Foundation decided I should do.'

'If that's the problem, I'll see if I can plead your case,' Morgan says. 'You may be able to work here with me.'

Bray snorts. 'Farming? Think I'll pass.'

Morgan glares down at him. 'It puts food in front of you.'

'Yeah, you'd just love to be able to keep me on a tight leash. I'd have even less freedom if I worked here.'

'Is that what you think I want?' Morgan places his hands on the table and leans over. 'You listen to me. We promised your parents we'd look after you, keep you safe, and make sure you have everything you need to live a good life. I'm pretty damn sure smuggling guns wasn't what they had in mind.'

'Mum and Dad wouldn't have cared what I was doing. They were too busy being anywhere but here.'

'You haven't got a clue what you're talking about.'

Bray shoves his chair back, knocking it onto the stone floor. 'Of course I don't! What the hell would I know? I'm only the one who lost my brother and my parents. I'm the one who was shoved all over the place because my parents were anywhere in the Sector but with me.'

Shayla tries to take his arm, but he pulls away from here. 'Don't! I'm going to my room. Let me know when I can come out again.' Bray ignores Morgan's shouts behind him as he storms up the stairs. He slams his door behind him and paces the wooden floor at the foot of his bed. Every single argument between himself and Morgan ends the same way. His parent's certain disappointment in him is continuously shoved in his face. Either that or he is compared to his dead brother. If Bray has to hear "If Daegan was alive blah, blah, blah" one more time he'll probably do something he'll seriously regret. How does Morgan expect him to get anywhere if he's being held back by a ghost?

Bray shouts and kicks the leg of his bed.

'Don't take your bad mood out on the furniture.'

Bray spins and glares at Morgan. 'Great, so I've no privacy either.'

Morgan opens his mouth to respond but restrains himself. He leans against the doorframe and rubs his forehead. 'I love you like a son, Bray. You know that, right?'

Bray slumps on to the end of his bed. 'Whatever. What's the but?'

'I can't do this anymore, Bray. Heaven knows, we've tried — for your sake and to honour Maggie, but we're done.'

Bray's stomach drops. 'What do you mean?'

'You're booked on the next transport to Vana.'

Bray stares at his uncle, not sure if he heard him right. His father's parents live on the small world on the border with the Foundation. It consists of a handful of settlements and a solitary transport hub. It is barely more than a retirement settlement. Whatever he feels about living on Earth, Vana is a hell of a lot worse. 'I'm sorry, okay.'

Morgan shakes his head. 'Too little too damn late. How many times have we been here before? It's becoming a weekly ritual.' Morgan holds up his hand as Bray opens his mouth to speak. 'And don't insult me by promising things will be different, that you won't get in trouble again. Living with us... it's not doing anyone any good. You're clearly miserable here and, to top it all off, your behaviour is affecting those around you. Officer Alder was moved from his position because his superiors found out he'd been going easy on you.'

Bray looks away from his uncle. Mace Alder had been decent to him. He didn't know the security officer had gotten in trouble for keeping him out of the system.

'Nothing to say about that? Mace was good to you and you don't have the decency to even pretend to give a damn. '

'You're only bothered what the neighbours think. Bet next door was on to Shayla the second she saw the transport dropping me off.'

'Don't try to twist this around. You know I couldn't care less about what other small-minded people think, but when it is hurting Shayla and Erin, I'm not going to turn a blind eye. You may not want to be here, but we do. We have to live here and the last thing we need is the Foundation or the Council breathing down our necks because you're always in trouble. The next stop for you is Tyrat and I'll be damned if I just sit back and do nothing while you head in that direction. Pack your things. Transport leaves in thirty minutes.'

Morgan turns and leaves without another word. Bray stares at the closed door, trying to understand what just happened. Once his brain kicks into gear he goes over to the window, ready to make his escape, but Morgan is way ahead of him. Morgan and three of their neighbours are standing guard outside. Morgan glances up, holds his gaze for a few seconds, then looks away.

Bray slumps onto the bed and looks around his room. He doesn't want to leave. Despite what he said, he does like living here. It's just the rigid Foundation rules he objects to. From a young age, he knew he had to work in Foundation HQ as an assistant to the Council. Not exactly the edge of your seat, exciting life he wants. For as long as he can remember, he's been fascinated with how things work. Most of his groundings were a result of him taking something apart he shouldn't have. Running after an overweight Foundation official is his worst nightmare.

Bray looks over at the photo on the wall. It was taken when he was an innocent four-year-old. He's sitting on his father's knee while Daegan is being tickled by their mother. The family looks relaxed and happy. It's just a pity he was too young to clearly remember anything about his brother. His anger quickly resurfaces as he stares at the picture. His brother probably would have slipped into his well-designed position in the Foundation. Daegan was the perfect child after all. The way people spoke of him you'd swear he never did anything he shouldn't have.

Well, Bray's not going to do what everyone else wants him to. Instead of seeing this as an exile, he's going to take full advantage. He'll do what he's told for a few weeks, earn his grandparents' trust, then make his escape. Vana's location on the border makes it the perfect place to disappear from. He's sure he can find transport to take him to the Outer Sector.

With a new purpose and focus in mind, Bray hurriedly packs a few things in a bag. If his family doesn't want him, he'll just have to find somewhere else he can call home.

ARES

Rayde stops outside the training room, his hand on the door controls. 'You know I said sometimes we have to make difficult decisions for the good of the Nomad.'

'Yes.'

'Well, I recently found out one of our own has been planning to remove me from my position. It seems he's not happy about you being on the ship. Been trying to undermine me.'

Gryffin frowns as he looks at the door. He knows many people don't like him being here but can't think of which of those would want to take Rayde's job.

'I need you to go in there and make sure he can't

hurt the Nomad. Make an example of him. Do you understand? Only one of you leaves that room.'

It takes a few seconds for the realisation to hit Gryffin. 'Kill him? You want me to kill a Nomad?'

'Survival of the Nomad as a group is the most important thing. You understand that, right?'

Gryffin nods. 'Yes, but-'

'Your job on this ship is to make sure the Nomad remain strong. That no one tries to undo what we've worked so hard to achieve. Anyone who tries to destroy us is shown no mercy. It's what you've been training for. It's what I need you to do. You do want to stay on board, don't you?'

Gryffin nods again, but he feels far from happy about what Rayde is saying. He wants to stay on the ship though. 'Who is it?'

Instead of answering, Rayde opens the door and gestures for him to enter. Creed is gagged and hanging by his arms from the railing running around the training room. His face is bruised and bleeding, but his look is defiant as ever as he meets Gryffin's eyes. 'Sir-'

'I'm giving you an order, Gryffin. I expect you to follow it.' Without another word, Rayde walks out and closes the door behind him. Gryffin rubs his palm against his leg and stares at the closed door, hoping Rayde will open it again and let him out. He doesn't want to kill Creed. He's been part of his life as long as Rayde has. But if he betrayed Rayde he deserves to be punished. That's the way things work. You do something wrong, you get punished. Defying orders is no different. He has to do what Rayde ordered him to do or he risks being punished too.

He slowly turns towards the bound Nomad and takes a deep breath. Creed keeps his eyes locked on Gryffin as he walks down the spiral stairs to the lower level. As Gryffin gets closer he can see blood on the man's bare chest and arms. Whatever happened, Creed had put up a fight. He wouldn't have expected anything less. He had never fought him but he'd seen him fight often. The man was one of the best.

With only a few years between them, Creed was the Nomad he looked up to the most - even above Rayde. Creed was fearless, strong, well respected and well-liked. Something Gryffin could only dream of being, and while Rayde was respected, Gryffin isn't so sure he's liked. Being liked is sometimes compared to being weak, but Gryffin knows that's not the case. No one could call Creed weak. Gryffin licks his dry lips and meets Creed's cool blue eyes.

Creed locks his knees and stands upright, taking pressure from his bruised and bloodied arms. Gryffin reaches up and pulls the gag from Creed's mouth. He knows there are no cameras in here so Rayde won't be watching him.

'So you can think for yourself? Rayde won't be happy about that.' His voice is hoarse but firm.

'Why did you betray Rayde?'

Creed laughs then spits out some blood. 'Betrayal, huh?' He shakes his head. 'Yeah, makes sense he'd go for that one.'

'What are you talking about?'

'I'm not going to waste the little time I have left by trying to explain it to you.'

'I need you to explain it. Why does Rayde want me to kill you?'

'I questioned him one too many times.'

'About what?'

Creed laughs and wipes his bloody face on his arm. 'About you of course.'

'Me?'

'Wake up, Gryffin. He's training you to be a weapon. Can't you see that? All this stuff about hiding your emotions, using whatever the hell is in your head. It's not right. It'll backfire on you and the Nomad. Sooner or later, you'll destroy all of this. You won't mean to but it'll happen. And it'll be his fault. So I told him that. And here I am.'

'I'll talk to him.'

Creed laughs again. 'You're embarrassing yourself.' He closes his eyes and sucks in a breath. 'You don't have a choice but to kill me. Can you not see that? You'll never have a choice again.' He laughs harshly. 'You know, I actually feel sorry for you. You've gone from one prison to another one. Or will unless you wake up and see what's going on.'

Gryffin is lost.

'Do I have to spell it out for you. Stand up for yourself. Rayde gave you a second chance. But all you're doing is what he's telling you to do. That sound right to you?'

'He's the captain.'

'That doesn't mean you can't think for yourself, Gryffin. That doesn't mean you become what he wants you to be. I may think you're more trouble than you're worth, but using you like this is wrong. You've got to put a stop to it before it goes too far. You hear me?'

Gryffin nods, but can't fully see what Creed is talking about. 'I'm-'

'Don't you dare disgrace the Nomad by apologising for what you're going to do. It's bad enough I don't get to go down fighting like a Nomad. Don't dishonour me by saying another damn word. Understood?'

Gryffin pauses then pulls at the chain securing Creed to the railing. It gives way, dumping Creed on the floor in a heap. He winces as he pushes himself to his knees. 'What the hell are you doing?'

Gryffin hands him one of the metal sparring sticks. 'Fair fight.'

Creed stares at the stick for a few seconds before he reaches out and lets Gryffin pull him to his feet. 'You're going to piss Rayde off.'

He shakes his head. 'Only one of us will leave by the door.'

'Can't ask for more than that.' He groans as he takes a few steps away from Gryffin. 'Remember what I said, okay?'

'I will.'

Less than ten minutes later Gryffin drags Creed's battered and bloody body out of the lift and along the corridor leading to the cargo hold. Nomad freeze as he squeezes past with their former commander. He lowers the body to the side of the door, next to the loading ramp then turns to the three Nomad staring at him. 'Get out of here.'

They don't move, each one looking at Creed's body at Gryffin's feet.

'He's going out the airlock. You want to join him?'

Without waiting for an answer, he pulls a tarp from the rack on the bulkhead and lies it on the ground. He lifts Creed's body onto it and rolls it up. The door to the hangar rattles shut as the men make a hasty exit. Gryffin looks down at Creed. A strange hollow ache forms in his stomach as he realises this is it. There's no going back from what he did. Creed is gone and nothing he does or says can undo that. Once Rayde made his decision there was nothing anyone could have done. At least the Nomad got to finish his time on *Ares* fighting. Better than hanging from the walkway in the training room.

He finishes what he's doing then loads the rest of the crates with the delivery of scrap metal. A freighter is due to collect the shipment within the hour. After getting rid of the crew assigned to the task, it leaves him to finish what they started. Once everything is where it should be, he pulls the tarp into the smaller loading bay to the side and seals it inside. He stands at the door and watches as the tarp is ejected into space and floats away from *Ares*.

Gryffin checks the crates again, making sure everything is sealed correctly. Before he gets to the door, he stops and looks back at the shipment then at the airlock. 'Captain, Creed has been taken care of. I spaced the body.' He shuts off his comms and walks away.

16

Brayden crouches behind the tree and watches his prey through the sight on his grandfather's old-fashioned rifle. He's been tracking his prey since just before sunrise and is getting closer. Ever since he was exiled here on Vana by Morgan, the desert landscape has been his playground. It's the only place he's been able to find peace. He loves his grandparents, but he can't stand being on this barren rock. The years he spent here with his parents was long enough. The last thing he wants is to waste years of his life here again. There's nothing on the rock. That's probably why it was so attractive to his parents. Foundation law stated they couldn't be together. His brother was born out of wedlock and his father remained a mystery. A big no-no in the eyes of the Foundation. If he was thinking rationally, he would have asked why his mother never mentioned who Daegan's father was. Why the big secret? What was so special about his brother's mystery father that he had to be kept a big secret? Bray couldn't care less. Well, deep down he wanted to know but he wasn't going to show interest. All he knew is that thanks to Daegan - yet again - his parents had to make sacrifices. He had to make sacrifices.

Bray kicks the rock at his feet, yelping as he bruises his toe. Yeah, he'll happily blame that on Daegan too. Remembering why he's here in the first place, he targets the boar, silently thanking his lucky stars it didn't scarper away when he stubbed his toe.

The giant beast and its equally impressive tusks has been dodging him for the last two weeks. Today that ends. There's enough meat on it to last the three of them weeks. It escaped from a neighbour's farm so, as far as Bray is concerned, it's fair game.

If he doesn't get it today, he's going to be in a world of trouble when he gets home. Instead of taking the last of his end of year exams, he's tracking this boar.

He slowly raises the gun and points at the beast's heart. Just before he takes his shot he hears his name being called out. He closes his eyes biting back a curse as the boar charges into the ravine. He slowly stands up and looks towards his grandfather, standing a few metres from him. 'Thanks, Pop. I had him.'

His grandfather stuffs his hands in the pockets of his olive green pants and makes a face as he looks at the ground. 'Not sure the beast deserved to die by your hand.'

'What's that supposed to mean?'

'He's a fine animal. Something like that should go by the hand of someone who tells the truth. Someone who doesn't throw what small semblance of a future he has left away so he can scramble around in the dirt.'

Bray sighs as he packs up his gun. 'Thanks for the pep talk, Pops. Real inspirational.'

'Speaking of inspirational, do you know where I spent the afternoon? I was in a meeting at the school. Sit down.'

Bray looks around him. 'Where exactly?'

'Sit your ass down on the dirt, Brayden and shut your mouth for once.'

Bray sighs and drops down onto the dusty ground. His grandfather crouches down in front of him. He may be in his eighties, but the man is still as formidable as ever. His grey hair was thinning, the lines on his face more pronounced, but his brown eyes are as sharp. 'What the hell is going on in your head, boy, huh?'

'Nothing.'

'That's hitting the nail on the head. Did you honestly think you'd get away with it?'

Bray shrugs.

'That's it, huh. You break into your teacher's office. Search through his paperwork. Copy the answers to the exam then sell them at a premium to your mates. Ingenious plan apart from one small detail. Did you not think he'd get the hint something was wrong when his entire class got every answer correct? I mean, if the lot of you had a brain cell between you, we'd be in serious trouble.

'I didn't get full marks.'

'Aren't you the clever one. Just made enough mistakes so no one would get suspicious. Problem is, you didn't realise Leren has a camera in his office. One he fitted after the last time you pulled this stunt. Seriously, Brayden. If I had more hair, I'd be pulling it out. You're giving every credit back to the poor fools you sold the answers to.'

'Pops-'

'Don't you pops me. First thing tomorrow.'

Bray scowls at the dirt between his boots. 'Fine.'

'And you can drop that attitude.'

His grandfather laughs and runs his hand through the dirt. 'Me and your nan - we're happy here. God knows Foundation life wouldn't suit us. But you... Bray, your mother, your father, they wanted so much more for you. You did everything you could think of to piss Morgan and Shayla off and now you're doing a fine job of following suit with us. I'm damned if I know why.'

Bray doesn't want the guilt to take hold, but it catches a firm hold of his gut. 'I don't know, okay. I guess I'm just bored.'

'Of course you damn well are, you stupid boy.'

Bray frowns as he stares at his grandfather. 'What?'

'You're one of the smartest people I know, Bray. Why the hell do you think I see red when you pull cock-eyed stunts like this? Fighting last week. Stealing this week. I've no proof but I'm damn sure you were the one who broke into the gunmakers shed and made off with a box of handguns. There were probably sold to that Rogue transport that landed about a month ago. Someone with half a brain would have jumped at the chance to sell them to someone leaving the surface.'

Bray focuses on the bug climbing up his boot. He knows his lack of response is all the confirmation his pops needs.

'Thought as much. I don't understand what your problem is. All we're asking you to do is take a few exams - without cheating. That's all it'll take, then you can leave this rock and make a place for yourself.'

'In the Foundation.'

His grandfather snorts and shakes his head. 'Thought I just said you were the smartest person I know. Why would you follow that with such an idiotic statement? Of course not with the Foundation.'

'What?'

'You can go anywhere. Be anything. The Foundation won't allow that. Finish your exams, get a ship and go find yourself.'

'Oh, so you want rid of me too.'

'If I didn't have to get up I'd slap you across the head. Of course we don't want that. But we don't want you to let your life flitter away like it is. You may think

I'm a clueless old man, but I know where you're heading. You escaped a trip to a juvenile detention centre on Earth although I can't for the life of me figure out how you did that. That guard Mace must have created some piece of fiction with your record. You don't have that here. If they find out you took those guns, you're in prison. No question. Leren is only allowing you resit the exams because we're old friends. He was all for expelling you and reporting you for theft. Keep heading this way and you'll throw the rest of your life away.'

'I know, okay.'

'Listen Bray, I know you're angry and I know you're hurting. As much as your nan and I would love to, there's damn all we can do to fix that. All I can say is that Morgan, Shayla, Erin, your nan and I... we're all hurting too. Daegan disappearing like that... it set this family on a path we can't come off. It's not too late for you though. You're still alive. You've got to stop whatever the hell it is you're doing. You hear me?'

Bray nods. 'Yeah. I hear you.'

'Good. Now help me up before I seize up for good.'

Bray smiles and helps him to his feet. They walk side by side back to the house on the top of the hill. From the front porch, he can see most of the town spread out below them. His grandfather settles into his rickety rocking chair and waves his hand at Bray. 'Get me a drink. And see if your nan needs any help. Might as well take advantage of you while you're still around.' He winks at Bray and closes his eyes, rocking himself gently.

He finds his nan in the kitchen, busy preparing dinner. She smiles at him before focusing on the vegetables again. 'So, I presume Hugh set the record straight with you?'

'Yes. I get it, okay. I messed up.'

'Is that all you got from his little talk with you?'

Bray drops onto the wooden chair and picks up one of the pea pods off the table. He shells it, popping the juicy peas into his mouth. 'No. I got it all. I'll talk to Leren tomorrow. I'll give the credits back.'

His nan grunts and turns away, but he sees her smile in the reflection in the window. 'Glad to hear it. Feed the dog will you? Then bring Hugh a beer. Chasing you halfway across the town is thirsty work.'

Bray kisses his nan on the forehead as he passes, calling the dog onto the back porch. He tips the meal into the old chocolate Labrador's bowl, scratches him behind the ear, then pulls a bottle from the cooler before wandering around to the front of the house. 'Got your beer, Pops.'

His grandfather ignores him, staring ahead towards the town.

Bray sighs. 'I'll talk to Leren tomorrow, okay. It's all good.'

He nudges his grandfather on the shoulder, but instead of turning and giving him an earful, he slides sideways in the chair. The bottle crashes to the deck as Bray releases it from his hand. He takes two steps closer and his breath catches in his throat. Pops eyes are open, staring blankly at the ground in front of the porch. Dinner finished, the dog nudges Pop's hand and whines. Bray crouches down in front of his grandfather and buries his face in the dog's chocolate coat as he screams to himself.

17

'You sure you don't want the standard design?'

Gryffin shakes his head even though he does want the standard Nomad design. Every Nomad he's met has the swirling black lines tattooed onto him. Rayde wanted something different for him though. In the ten years since he was rescued, he's looked to Rayde for guidance on everything. He knows he's unpredictable and that's why he's spent most of that time either alone or with Rayde, but now he's beginning to get control of himself he thought he'd be allowed to become a proper Nomad, not just used to enforce Rayde's leadership.

It seems Rayde has other ideas. He wants Gryffin to have his namesake covering half his back, his left arm and half his chest. The tattoo is going to be huge. He doesn't want there to be any doubt who Gryffin is - not that there would be. The metal components make him stand out as it is. He's letting his hair grow longer to partially hide his facial implant. Rayde hasn't mentioned anything about it yet so he'll leave it that way until he's told otherwise. He wants to blend in, but Rayde is doing whatever he can to make Gryffin stand out.

Gryffin nods at Ryder. 'Do it.'

Ryder nods and gestures to the bed in front of him. Gryffin pulls off his top and lies down. 'It's gonna be big. Probably take the rest of the day. Maybe few more hours in a week or so.'

'All of it in one go.'

Ryder's eyes open a little wider but he has the good sense not to argue. 'It's your body.' Ryder pauses for a few seconds. 'What do you want to do about the brand on your back?'

'Go over it.'

'The ink probably won't cover it entirely.'

'Just go over it.'

Ryder stops asking questions and gets on with it. Gryffin barely feels the tattoo needle on his skin. Getting inked should be a rite of passage for each Nomad. It meant they're officially a part of the crew. Gryffin doesn't feel happy or proud though. He's only getting it because he killed Creed. He doesn't want to be honoured for that. Every time he looks at the damn tattoo he's going to be reminded of what he did to Creed. The Commander was just looking out for him. He shouldn't have paid for that with his life. No changing that. It's something Gryffin's going to have to live with... and remember every time he sees the tattoo.

18

Bray wipes blood from his eye and smiles at his opponent. The trader is about five years older than him. He keeps telling himself that's just a coincidence... again. The trader is flagging. His blows losing strength. Bray just needed to hang on a little longer and he'd win.

Bray lunges while the other man is catching his breath. His fist connects with his jaw, snapping the man's head to the side. Bray's right fist drives into the trader's stomach, sending him to the floor gasping for breath. Bray lunges again, but the trader holds up his hand, forfeiting the fight. Not the win Bray wanted but it's a win. The crowd cheers and credits exchange hands.

He pushes his sweat soaked hair from his face and looks at the figures on the betting board. He should made quite a bit from the fight.

Or would have if the Vana security group hadn't taken that moment to burst through the doors. Spectators and fighters alike scramble for any available exit, but they don't get far. All the exits are covered. Pretty impressive for a group of locals with minimal training. Bray doesn't bother trying to make a run for it. He couldn't even if he wanted to. The organiser locks the fighting cage to make sure the fighters can't change their mind and leave mid fight. Bray sits in the centre of the blood splattered floor and watches the security force gather up everyone outside the ring.

It takes about half an hour before a squat man approaches the cage. He shakes his head as he looks down at Bray lying on the floor with his hands behind his head. 'Why am I not surprised to see you here?'

'Hey Leren. Didn't know you volunteered?'

His teacher clasps his hands together in front of him. 'Helps to pay the bills. Not everyone makes a living out of selling exam results. What are you doing in there?'

Bray pushes himself up to his elbows. 'Helps to pay the bills.'

Leren sighs and shakes his head. 'I've called your grandmother. She'll meet us at the courthouse.'

'Court?'

'Yes, Bray. Court. This is an illegal fighting ring. You wilfully signed up to fight. You're facing a sentence for that.'

Bray nods, trying not to let the realisation of a jail sentence show on his face.

Leren unlocks the cell and gestures for Bray to get up. He fixes restraints around his wrists and leads him out of the building to the waiting transport.

The journey to the courthouse goes by in a blur. Bray refuses to let himself think about what's going to happen. He just wanted to fight. The pay was good and so were the contacts. After his pops died three months ago, he tried to do the right thing, but he couldn't stick to it. Life was tough on Vana. They'd been struggling to survive. His Nan never said anything. But he's not an idiot. Taking his exams wasn't going to put food on the table. Fighting. Stealing and reselling to visiting off-world traders. That did. Over the last few months, he'd earned enough to make sure his Nan could afford three meals a day for a few months at least.

He's dragged out of the transport and brought into the courthouse. Being caught in the act meant he was guilty. No need for a defence or dragging things out. He'd be sentenced immediately.

His Nan covers her mouth and gasps when she sees him. She hurries over and wipes tears from her eyes. 'What have you been doing? You're covered in blood.'

'You know the creaky board on the back porch?'

She frowns and nods. 'What does that-'

'Push it aside. There's a box inside. Code is 461978. Everything in there is for you.'

'I don't understand.'

'Do you remember the code?'

'Yes. Bray-'

The judge arrives and Bray is led away from her. Bray barely listens as the charges are read out and he is sentenced to six months in the juvenile facility an hour away. He can do six months. There's enough credits in the box under the porch to last his Nan that long.

He smiles at her, hating that she's still crying for him. 'Love you.' He doesn't hear her reply as he is taken out of the room and into the transport.

PART 6

2 YEARS LATER

GRYFFIN – 23 YEARS OLD
BRAY – 18 YEARS OLD

VANA

Bray crouches down in front of the two graves and places a flower on each one. He loosens his tie as he rises to his feet again. The rest of the funeral party had moved back to the house for food and drinks, but Bray couldn't think of anything worse than mixing with a group of people to reminisce and tell stories. His grandmother is dead. There's nothing else to talk about. She went to bed to read and didn't wake up again.

He squints against the searing sun as he looks around the spartan landscape of Vana. He should have stuck to his original plan and left this dump two years ago, but things didn't work out that way. Story of his fucking life. Even though he hated the place, he couldn't leave his grandmother alone. She took him in when no one else wanted him. The least he could do is look after her when she needed him. Now that she's gone...

He turns and looks back at the town. His grandparent's house... his house now sits on a small rise at the far end of town. Shayla, Morgan and Erin are there right now. Things between Bray and Morgan had deteriorated further. Morgan was furious at him. He can't blame him. The initial six months for illegal fighting had stretched to a year for bad behaviour. Continuing to fight while being incarcerated for that very offence hadn't done him any favours. The credits he won from the other inmates for the fights had made the extra time worth it. Those credits had gone straight to his Nan when he got out.

It may not have been Tyrat Prison Moon but the year in the facility had gotten to him. He thought he was tough, but constantly watching your back in case someone stuck a knife it would take its toll on anyone. Over the year he'd traded nearly half his winnings from the weekly fights in exchange for alcohol and drugs. Anything to take the edge off the fear, off the loneliness, off the shame. That all ended as soon as he got out. He needed to prove to himself that he was strong. The drink he could control, it was the drugs that refused to release their hold so easily. Nearly a year later the addiction is still kicking his ass, but he'd get through it.

Since getting out, he'd done everything he could to make sure he could support his Nan. The tricky part was avoiding getting arrested again. So far, he'd been lucky, but it was only a matter of time.

He looks in the other direction at the small spaceport then back at the house before turning back to his grandparents' graves. There's nothing left on Vana for him. Apart from a handful of traders he owes money to, no one is going to miss him. He's exhausted all his contacts. Local traders knew to avoid him and had increased their security in case he took a liking to what they were selling. There's nothing on Earth for him either. Shayla and Morgan made it clear he's a bad influence on Erin and he's not welcome - well, not until he sorts himself out. Since he came out here full-time, he hasn't done much to get himself on the right track. If anything, he'd pretty much put both feet firmly on the one going slightly askew.

He looks back up at the house on the hill and sighs. His family are waiting up there for him. No doubt Morgan has a lecture or two up his sleeve brimming with disappointment and unhelpful comparisons to 'can't-do-no-wrong' Daegan. A large part of him yearns for one of Shayla's comforting hugs, but facing the whole town is bad enough without adding Morgan to the mix.

He places his hands over his face, resisting the urge to scream in frustration. When had everything gone so very wrong for him? What had he done to deserve having everyone he's ever loved taken from him one after the other? Who'd be next? He lets his hands drop to his sides. As much as he hates Morgan, if anything happened to him, Shayla or Erin… He shakes his head, trying to dislodge the dark thoughts from his mind. He couldn't cope with that. Losing his brother was bad enough without adding his parents years later.

His fists tighten as the familiar anger builds. People have told him it's irrational and unfair, but he's not strong enough to control his feelings. If Daegan hadn't begged and begged to go on that trip, he wouldn't have disappeared without a trace. If that didn't happen, Bray's parents wouldn't have spent the rest of their short lives trying to find him. Daegan's selfishness destroyed the family. Bray can never forgive him for that. He'd love to be able to tell him to his face what he'd done. To tell him how he'd managed to mess things up for everyone, but he can't even do that. Bray would have to carry around his hatred for the rest of his life. He'd have to live knowing he could never live up to the memory of his dead brother. Morgan would always be disappointed and Shayla… He squeezes his eyes shut. He'd have to get used to seeing that look on her face every time he did something he shouldn't.

Bray freezes for a moment as a realisation hits him. He looks down at the graves and smiles. 'I'm sorry I let you guys down. I love you both and will always be grateful for everything you did for me. But I have to go. You know that, right?'

With one last look over his shoulder at the house on

the hill, Bray turns towards the spaceport and his new life – as far away from his family and the memories as possible.

PART 7

2 YEARS LATER

GRYFFIN – 25 YEARS OLD
BRAY – 20 YEARS OLD

20

Bray brings the transport down to land on his allocated space and shuts the engine off. He peers out the cockpit, a heavy weight settling in his stomach. He hates this dump. Right on the edge of Foundation space, Nava Three is a breeding ground for all the dregs of society - Foundation and other colonies alike. For the most part, the Foundation left them alone to kill each other far away from their rules and regulations. A plus if you were in Bray's line of work.

When he left Vana he never planned to fall into his old habits again, but life had other plans for him. He looks over his shoulder at the crate of weapons in the hold of the shuttle. His nan and pops would have a thing or two to say about what he was doing. Morgan and Shayla too no doubt. After his nan died he tried damn hard to take a straighter path. Didn't last long though. Leaving Vana with no credits hadn't been his brightest move. Selling what he stole at the port had paid for his fare off Vana. After that, he did whatever he had to do to survive. His shuttle was paid for from reselling things that weren't his to sell. He gave up feeling guilty about it after the first month. His family may not approve but they weren't around to voice their disgust anymore. He wasn't letting them down - not any longer. It was just him, alone and living from day to day. From job to job.

Time to meet with Hardy and get his payment.

Bray pulls his hood up, trying to shield his face from the biting wind that howls through the narrow street. He's dealt with this customer before but that means fuck all out here. Your best mate would stab you in the back given half the chance. That's the main reason he works alone. Only one back to worry about.

He weaves, elbows, and shoves his way through the crowded streets, keeping his weapons and credits away from thieving hands. It takes about ten minutes to work his way to the centre of the town. He follows the thump of music to Hardy's bar. Instead of joining the growing line of punters, he walks straight up to the door. A brute of a man blocks the entrance, his arms crossed over his chest. Bray glances at his arms before looking back at his face. Each arm is the size of Bray's leg. 'Bray. Hardy is expecting me.'

The man checks his handheld, grunts then steps aside, giving Bray just enough room to squeeze by, closing the door behind him. A wall of hot air hits Bray like a physical blow. He pulls down his hood and runs a hand through his hair.

A woman in a booth just inside the door gazes lazily up at him. 'Weapons.'

'No thanks. I've got my own.'

Joke lost on her, she repeats her statement. 'Weapons.'

Bray raises his eyebrows then reaches into his coat, pulling the two guns out. She gives him a ticket, locking his weapons into a metal locker behind her.

'Great to enjoy your work, isn't it.'

Nothing from her again. She's either too high on something or he's seriously losing his touch. Following the noise, and the smell of far too many less-than-clean bodies, he takes the door at the end of the corridor and leans over the top of the metal staircase. Below him, a mass of bodies swells in time to the ear-splitting music blaring from speakers embedded in the ceiling. Most of the punters are keeping some form of time with the music but there are too many moving to their own beat. Below him, he catches a group of men helping themselves to bright yellow pills from one of the barkeeps. He recognises the drug from his time at the prison on Vana. He'd lost too many nights to the stuff while he was incarcerated. He'd fought to escape the addiction, but watching the pills being passed around the bar, he feels an unwelcome pull he thought he had a handle on.

A scantily clad woman gyrates over to him, drawing his attention from the bar and the pills. She runs her hand along his shoulders as she circles him. 'Haven't seen you here before,' she shouts in his ear. Bray keeps his arms tight to his side. He wants to leave here with all his credits and body parts still on his person.

Ignoring her, he extracts himself and descends into the throng of bodies. She follows him down the stairs but is quickly distracted by someone else who makes the mistake of making eye contact. Good luck to him.

Bray pushes through the crowd, making slow but steady progress across the room to the far side. The twin of the giant he met outside blocks his approach. 'Who the fuck are you?'

'Bray. Hardy is expecting me,' Bray repeats.

The man glares down at him as he reaches behind and opens the door. Still keeping him firmly in his sights, the bodyguard grants him entry to the room.

Hardy is sitting behind the ridiculously ornate desk sipping a dark liquid from a wide-rimmed glass. Bray's met her a few times, but it still hits him how out of place Hardy is on Nava Three. At a touch over six-foot-tall, well-built and well-bred, Elora Hardy is more suited to Foundation life than roughing it with the scum of society. Her thick blonde hair reaches to her waist and is braided and hanging over one shoulder. The shirt and trousers she wears are tailored - something you'd be hard pushed to find out here.

Hardy stands up and offers Bray her hand, her grip strong and sure. 'Long time, Bray.'

'I've been keeping busy.'

Hardy lowers into her chair and smiles, showing perfect teeth. 'So I hear. Making quite a name for yourself. Rumour has it you took out one of my rivals?'

Bray smiles. 'You don't want to believe everything you hear.'

Hardy laughs and offers him a drink, which he accepts. 'Well, whoever took him out did me a favour. I might be able to offer them a bonus.'

'What kind of bonus?'

She slides a glass of whiskey across the table and runs a perfectly manicured red nail around the rim of her glass. 'Well, let's think about this. I presume you got what I asked for?'

Bray nods and takes a sip of the whiskey. 'Whoa, that's damn good.'

'Of course,' Hardy responds with a sly grin. 'So? You have my order?'

'Of course,' he counters, earning a chuckle from his host.

'I never doubted you for a second. Well, if I were to... bump into whoever did me this favour, they could expect an additional twenty-percent above what we agreed.'

Hardy is fair but that's a hell of a bonus. 'Won't say no.'

She smirks. 'Didn't think you would. So, Tank will oversee the delivery. Once he signs off on the goods, he'll make the transfer. Same details as last time?'

Bray nods. 'Appreciate that.'

Hardy walks around the desk and sits in front of him. She crosses her legs and examines him closely. 'You look rough.'

Bray snorts. 'Cheers.'

'You still living in that wreck of a transport?'

'Hey, insult me but leave my home out of it.'

Hardy pulls his seat closer and straddles him. She places a finger under his chin and lifts his head. 'You're going to get yourself killed, you know that.'

'I'm doing okay. You this concerned about all your customers?'

'Only the ones I have a... certain interest in.' She proves her point by kissing him hard, digging her nails into his scalp as she pulls him close. She breaks the kiss. 'Don't move.'

'Wouldn't dream of it.'

She smiles as she stands up and reaches over to lock the door. She shrugs out of her expensive trousers and kisses him as she slowly opens his trousers. Hardy straddles him again and take a handful of his hair. She moves his head to the side and nips at his ear. 'Are you ready for your tip?'

Instead of answering, Bray lifts his hips and Hardy gasps. 'I guess you are.'

Bray grins. 'Stop talking.'

Once Hardy has finished "tipping" him Bray closes his eyes and lies back in the chair. Hardy taps him on the hand and he takes the glass of drink from her.

'Don't know what I did to deserve being tipped...twice, but I'm not complaining.'

Hardy lowers into her chair and straightens her shirt. 'The problem with you, Bray, is that you are too good-looking for my own good. If all my clients were like you I'd get nothing done. The last one I had in had no teeth and no personal hygiene.'

Bray empties his glass and places it on the table. 'Cut it out, Hardy. What's up?'

She crosses her legs and rests her hands on her knee. 'The Foundation and those vile guards from Tyrat have been sniffing around. I need to close this place down and rethink operations. Sorry, Bray, but this is it for us. My advice is to keep your head down and have a little rethink yourself.'

'Foundation is here?'

She shakes her head. 'Not yet. Don't think so anyway, but it's only a matter of time. Two days ago they were within spitting distance. I'm winding down operations - just until I find out what they're up to. I can't say I'm too keen on a stay in Tyrat. Don't want to shut this down, but I won't take the risk.'

She hands him another glass of whiskey. 'Not what I wanted to hear, but I get it. Where does that leave Nava?'

Hardy purses her lips. 'Hell if I know. I'll leave the club open, just shut down the... grey areas. I'm going to take myself away somewhere less...'

'Grey,' Bray finishes for her.

'Indeed. I am sorry, Bray. I know we're a big

customer.'

'I don't fancy Tyrat any more than you do. Like I said, I get it. Better get that shipment unloaded.'

'Hey, you could always tag along.'

'With you?'

'With me. You fancy leaving that stunning transport of yours behind and vanishing with me for a while.'

He thinks about it for less than a minute. Hardy is amazing, but he's not ready to give up just yet. He can make a go of this himself, he just needs a little more time. 'Tempting offer.'

She smiles and nods. 'But you've got to pass. I understand.' Hardy walks around the desk and sits in front of him. She combs her long fingers through his hair, brushing it back from his face. 'Such a shame we have to call quits to our relationship. I would have liked to see where it went.'

'You'd have killed me.'

'Not straight away.' She winks and smiles as she gets to her feet. Bray downs the last of the whiskey. He's going to miss the expensive alcohol. Hardy hugs him and takes her seat behind her desk again. 'You watch that beautiful back of yours.'

'You too, Hardy. And thanks - for everything.'

'If my situation changes, I'll find you. I can promise you that,' she winks and blows him a kiss. 'Tank will be ready whenever you are.' Bray closes the door behind him and turns to face the crowded dance floor. As soon as he steps forward, the dancers move to the side. He glances behind him, seeing the hulking form of Tank following him. No wonder the crowd got the hell out of the way.

Twenty minutes later, he shuts the door of the transport after Tank and checks the credits in his highly illegal and completely untraceable account. Hardy was true to her word. The extra twenty percent will help tide him over until he finds a new customer. He leans against the bulkhead and slams his fist into the ship. He was on to a good thing with Hardy. Unlike most of the people he dealt with, he could trust her. Without that steady, reliable income, he's fucked. The transport is refuelled but unless he's planning on landing somewhere and not moving for the rest of his life, that's not going to last long.

He could stay on Nava Three, look for another customer. That thought vanishes as he glances out the front of the transport. He feels dirty even being here. Time to go.

Bray dumps his coat on the console beside him and settles into the pilot seat. He has another shipment due for delivery in a little under thirty hours. Might as well head in that direction. He might get lucky and pick up another client there. If not, there's a chance he'll have to sell the transport to get by.

He closes his eyes and rests his head against the back of the seat. He could always go back to Vana. His grandparents' house is probably still empty, waiting for him to take over the farm. As hard as he tries, he can't see himself settling anywhere, let alone Vana.

There's nothing left there for him since they died.

Thoughts of Morgan, Shayla and Erin follow as always. It would be so easy to set a course for Earth, through various back doors, and go home. He hasn't spoken to any of them since the funeral. His position with the Foundation would probably still be open. In a few months, he could have a job, a future... and no freedom. He'd also be back under the shadow of Daegan.

Is that so bad though? At least he'd have security. He sighs and keys in a comms code into the panel in front of him. He clears his throat as he waits for the connection to lock.

'Hello?'

Morgan's voice echoes in the transport, instantly pulling him back to the old farmhouse. Bray opens his mouth but nothing comes out. He looks out the front of the ship and his resolve crumbles. What the hell is he doing? He's just sold illegal guns to an illegal trader on a shady colony.

'Hello? Who is it? I'm not a damn mind reader. You got to say something.'

Bray slams his fist into his leg and closes his eyes.

'Bray?'

He opens his eyes and stares at the comms panel. Morgan clears his throat and his voice softens. 'Bray? Is that you, boy? Are you okay?'

Bray reaches out and cuts the connection. It's too soon. Maybe in a few months. He clenches his trembling hand and curses himself. What the hell was he doing opening that wound again?

With one last look at Nava Three, he starts the ignition sequence and sets off, although not quite sure where to.

PART 8

2 YEARS LATER

GRYFFIN – 27 YEARS OLD
BRAY – 22 YEARS OLD

21

Gryffin steps off the transport and squints against the onslaught of sunlight. After spending months on *Ares*, his sensitive eyes struggle against the change in lighting. He pulls the hood of his jacket down, shielding his eyes as they do their best to adjust, but failing miserably. The scrap-yard runs in all directions as far as the eye can see. Everything from wiring to transports to full-blown battleships covers the desert, seemingly with no rhyme or reason. Gryffin turns around, his hands by his side ready to reach for his weapon if needed. He doesn't like the feel of the place. There are too many places to hide, too many things that can be used as weapons lying on the ground all around them. He clenches his gloved fists and looks over his shoulder at the rest of the team.

The six Nomad stand three to each side of him. It's his first time as team leader and he's determined not to let them or Rayde down. He checks the directions Rayde gave him before stuffing his unit in his jacket. He nods to the three standing to his left. 'You stay with the transport. The rest with me.' He takes the third track through the salvage, breathing a sigh of relief when everyone does as ordered.

He knows the Nomad with him complained to Rayde about being on the team. He can't blame them. After he was ambushed in the training room seven years ago, the control implant in his head had made his life hell. Attacking the crew once was bad enough. Nearly doing it again, and again, and again had made him a liability. If it wasn't for Rayde having his back, he knows the crew would have kicked him off the ship. He was losing his grip on the control implant at least once a month - sometimes more often. Rayde had reinforced one of the cells in the training room just for him. Somewhere safe to keep him caged until he could get control of himself again. Waking up in the cell with the stomach-twisting nausea is becoming a part of his life. The only upside is the searing pain he gets seconds before he goes on a rampage. It gives the crew time to lock him away like some crazy animal.

He thought the time in the lab couldn't be topped, but it seems the Scientist left more surprises for him.

Gryffin doesn't want to find out what else he stowed away in his body, ready to rear its ugly head.

He holds up his fist, stopping the group as he slowly turns his head to the left. He thought he heard a ship. He lowers his hand and they continue through the yard.

They follow the path through the yard, the sweltering heat and their black uniforms working together to make it damn uncomfortable. He ignores muted mutters of complaint from the men behind him. His own body is giving him enough to complain about without adding the heat to it. As usual, his wretched metal arm and the connectors in his flesh are battling against each other. The impact of his boots on the ground jars his metal arm, sending ripples of pain up what's left of the limb. For too long, the pain has kept him company, refusing to let up for one damn second. Whenever he woke, he hoped he would have adjusted to it, that somehow, during the few hours of sleep he managed to get, that his first moment of consciousness wouldn't be filled with pain.

As if trying to make this day worse, a blaring headache builds behind his eyes as a result of the unforgiving light. He balls his fists at his sides, determined not to drive one or both of them into his forehead. It probably didn't help that Rayde had kept him in the training room for the last two days straight. The constant battles with the drones had only been broken when Rayde himself joined in, along with any Nomad he could spare from ship duties. On top of the regular pain, every inch of Gryffin's body aches after the hours of harsh training. He is in desperate need of a few hours in his bunk after a trip to the mess hall.

He stops in front of the hut at the far end of the track. If it wasn't in pride of place at the end of the walkway, he would have assumed it was part of the scrap. Two short, round men lounge outside the door, drinks in hand as they stare at the group of Nomad.

'You must be Rayde's new pet.' He looks Gryffin up and down, seemingly unimpressed with what he sees. Getting no response, the man on the left nudges his companion. 'Guess he hasn't taught him how to talk yet.' He gets to his feet and gestures towards the door. 'Never mind. The credits will do all the talking we need. Guns are inside.' Without waiting for an invitation, Gryffin follows him into the hut. He holds a hand out to the side, two fingers raised. Two Nomad stay outside while the third steps inside with him.

The air inside the hut is hot, heavy and foul-smelling. The men walk over to a low table at the far side and pull a stained cover off it. The guns Rayde ordered are spread over the metal surface. Gryffin picks one up and examines it. It's well used, but so is everything on *Ares*. He had been ordered to take whatever was offered and get the hell out of there before the brothers changed their mind - which happens a lot according to Rayde.

'So, happy with the products?'

Gryffin gestures behind him and the Nomad with him pulls the bag off his shoulder. Gryffin throws the credits on the table. The brothers count the payment then nod. 'Pleasure doing business with you.'

They load the weapons and have just finished as the hut vibrates. The door crashes open as one of the Nomad he left outside bursts in. 'Slavers.'

Gryffin looks at the brothers. 'You do this?'

For the first time since they arrived, they look like they're taking him seriously. 'No way. We don't deal with Slavers.'

Gryffin goes to the door and peers out. He can hear the ship in the distance. 'Where is it?'

'Right where our ship is.'

So that means the other Nomad on his team are either dead or taken by the Slavers. 'With me.' He leads the three remaining Nomad through the scrap-yard.

Gryffin crouches down and peers through the window of the rusted transport just down from their transport. Three Slavers are standing in front of his crew. The Nomad are on their knees with their hands clasped behind their heads. Damn it. First trip off *Ares* as the team leader and he's managed to completely fuck it up. Worse still, it's not him in the shit - it's his team. He moves his hand to activate his comms to contact Rayde but stops. He got them into this mess. He's going to get them out of it... somehow.

Gryffin checks his gun, satisfied it'll fire when he needs it to. Kellyn leans closer to speak in his ear. 'Plan?'

Good question. Just a shame he doesn't have an

answer. Taking his pause to mean exactly what it is, the Nomad gestures to the men with them. 'With me. I'm not waiting for him to get us killed.'

'Don't move.'

Gryffin's order falls on deaf ears. He can do nothing except watch as the rest of his team leave him to it, disappearing around the corner. Kellyn has been a problem for Gryffin since he organised the ambush in the training room. It didn't matter what Rayde's punishment had been, there was nothing he could do to change his feelings about Gryffin. Not that Gryffin cared, he'd just prefer if Rayde kept them away from each other instead of putting him on Gryffin's team.

As usual, Kellyn has managed to make a bad situation worse. This will go down in Nomad history as how not to lead a team. Gryffin backs away from his viewpoint, not relaxing until he's around the corner and out of sight. He spins as gunfire sounds from somewhere to the left of him. Nomad gunfire. He ducks behind a cooling unit, cursing as Kellyn and the other Nomad are lead back to the rest of the group and forced to their knees. Restraints are fitted to their wrists and ankles before they are hauled to their feet and led back to the Slaver transport.

Using the salvage as a shield, Gryffin slowly makes his way towards the transport. He carefully picks his way through the scrap, moving up the pile so he can get a clearer view. Thick smoke rises above the mound of scrap to his right. Exactly where they left the Nomad transport. These Slavers are pissing him off. Three

Slavers stand guard at the three entry points as two more load his men onto their ship. He has no doubts strong Nomad fighters would earn them a hefty fee in one of the underground fighting pits.

Gryffin assesses his options. He's a damn good shot but his men are already inside the ship. If he takes out the guards the Slavers inside would take out his men. The only way he can think of to get all the Slavers in one go is to wait until they're inside.

Decision made, he slips off his jacket and gloves then works through the razor-sharp scrap to an outcropping about twenty or so feet above the ship. The main body of the old-style craft made up most of the mound he was climbing, but its wing was a near-perfect ledge.

He pulls himself along the wing on his stomach, wincing as every groan and creak seems to echo loudly in the yard. He keeps one eye on the transport as the guards step inside and the door seals. The engines splutter to life, an unhealthy plume of smoke spilling out from the twin exhausts on the top of the ship. Gryffin closes his eyes and releases his fragile hold on the implants. The stomach-churning spinning sensation threatens to send him off the edge of the wing. He digs his hands in until the sensation passes a few seconds later. He opens his now purple eyes and his vision sharpens, bringing his world into razor-sharp focus. As the ship lifts from the ground, Gryffin reaches the edge and rises to his feet. A refreshingly cool breeze ruffles his hair as he watches the craft move towards his position. He waits until it is below him then drops off the ledge.

22

Gryffin lands on the top of the transport and slides down the rounded roof. He digs his metal fingers into the edge of the exhaust vent and pulls himself up the side. Avoiding the thick black fumes pouring from the vent, he climbs over the top and crawls towards the twin engines near the front of the craft. He examines the plating covering the internal workings. Only one way to take it down. He rams his fist against the plating. Three punches later he breaks through.

The ship's engines release their last splutter as Gryffin's fist embeds itself in the inner workings of the engine. He looks over at the second engine but he doesn't need to take it out. It's already struggling to hold the craft in the air. The alarms scream to life as the ship circles around, trying to land before the engines give way. Gryffin hangs on to the edge of the ruined engine and leans over the side of the ship. He pulls at the door release, yanking it open. He swings inside, ramming his boots into a Slaver. Gryffin executes Slaver Two and Three before moving into the cockpit and dispatching the last of the crew. The attack is so quick the first Slaver body just hits the floor as he fires a round into the pilot's head. He braces himself against the ceiling as the craft hits the ground in a cloud of dust and engine smoke.

He relieves the Slavers of their weapons then puts a round in the nav system. The last thing they need is for help to arrive in response to an automated SOS. Not that he thinks the ship has an automated anything. He's impressed the thing got off the ground in the first place.

With all the Slavers dealt with, Gryffin goes back into the main cargo hold and looks at each of his team in turn. They're on the floor against the far wall, chained to a metal railing welded to the bulkhead. Apart from a few bruised faces and possibly bruised prides, they seem to be unharmed. He searches the pockets of the downed Slaver leader but finds no keys. Must be a fingerprint lock. Gryffin severs the thumb and forefinger from the man and presses each to the lock. The thumb does the trick, releasing the chains. He unlocks each of his men, leaving Kellyn chained up.

He crouches down in front of him, targeting him with his purple eyes. Sweat gathers on the man's brow and drips into his eye. It's damn hot in the transport. Or maybe he's nervous. He should be. Gryffin clenches his teeth as his grip on the implant threatens to break.

'I get you don't want me on the crew. I know you don't trust me.'

'I don't-'

Gryffin levels his gun on Kellyn. 'Shut the fuck up. You don't have to like me. What you do have to do is follow my orders. Nothing else. I was never going to leave the surface without every single Nomad. Do you understand?'

Kellyn nods and swallows deeply. 'Understood, sir.'

Gryffin drops the thumb on the ground in front of him and steps out of the ship. As he passes the group of freed Nomad he gestures over his shoulder. 'Unlock him.'

Gryffin closes his eyes and takes a long, deep breath as he fights to rein in the implant. Sensation returns to his body, bringing with it the ever-present headache and ache in the flesh attached to the implants. He opens his eyes and blinks a few times, his vision blurring slightly as his eyes change back. In the distance, smoke still clouds the air where the Nomad ship once sat. If they're going to get off this rock they'll need to find themselves alternative transport. *Ares* won't be back for another few hours. Even then, the rendezvous isn't on the surface. He could call her back sooner than planned. Return to the ship empty-handed. Worse than that - minus a mode of transport and with their reputation in shreds. The Arta Brothers would take a little too much pleasure from spreading the word about what happened. No, the only option is to take back control of this mess. By force.

'Clear the Slaver crew of all weapons then destroy the ship. I don't want anything salvaged from it. Kellyn, you're with me.'

He hesitates, clearly less than thrilled about some one-on-one time with Gryffin, but changes his mind when Gryffin takes his gun out of his holster again. 'You want to disobey a second time?'

Kellyn follows Gryffin through the scrap yard towards their transport. They slow as the cloud of black smoke comes into view. Slavers had done a real number on the transport. Capturing a Nomad crew must be more profitable than salvaging the ship. Gryffin signals for Kellyn to stop while he checks the area. No sign of anyone. Gryffin moves around the edge of the space, keeping the shelter of the mounds of scrap at his back.

Time to see what the Arta's have to say about it. It takes less than five minutes to get to the Arta's shack. The two rusted metal chairs outside are empty. Kellyn follows Gryffin around the back. The chipped wooden door hangs open, the hinges creaking as the door swings in the gentle breeze. Gryffin signals to Kellyn and the Nomad peers around the door frame. He gives the all-clear and Gryffin steps inside. The heavy curtain separating the living area from the public side of the shop is drawn.

The back wall of the space is lined with row after row of weapon, securely chained to the wall. From a cursory glance, this is what Gryffin was sent here to collect. The Arta's didn't waste any time putting the weapons back into their stock. He points to the curtain and the two Nomad approach, testing each step on the groaning floorboards before they put their weight down. Gryffin slips a finger through the gap between the curtain and the wall, pulling it back enough to see through. The brothers are sitting behind their desk, a large pile of credits in front of them. The smaller of the two is counting while the other bags the payment. But payment for what? The Nomad crew? The guns Gryffin was meant to buy? The destroyed Nomad transport?

Right now, it doesn't matter. He looks at Kellyn, seeing a resolve in the Nomad's face. He's up for this as much as Gryffin. Gryffin mouths, three, two, one. On one the two men burst out from behind the curtain. Before they know what's going on, Kellyn has a gun jammed into the back of each man's head. Gryffin steps around the desk and glances at the front door to the shack. It's double locked. There won't be any interruptions.

'What the hell is going on? How did you get in here?'

'Back door's open.'

The smaller brother scowls at his sibling. 'You were meant to lock that!'

'I thought you said you would?'

Gryffin slams his mental fist onto the table, splitting the wood in two. Credits spill onto the ground, some of them slipping down between the floorboards. 'Slavers your idea?'

'What? No.'

'Key to the guns.'

'Now, let's be reasonable. You haven't paid for that many.'

'Key or he shoots you.'

The smaller brother fumbles in his pocket and holds the key out in a shaky hand. Kellyn takes it from him and pulls a sack from the pile in the corner. Leaving Gryffin with the men, he pulls the curtain aside and begins to fill the sacks.

Gryffin gestures to the credits littering the floor. 'Helped yourself to our payment.'

The larger brother laughs nervously. 'It's nothing personal. Got to take what you can when you can. Am I right?'

The top of his head disappears in a crimson halo as Gryffin puts a round in it. The smaller Arta brother screams as his brother's blood and brain matter splatters over the side of his face. 'Did you call in the Slavers?'

'No, no, I swear. Slavers… you can't trust them. Stab you in the back first chance they get.'

'So it was just a coincidence?'

'I don't know what they were doing here. Slavers haven't been here for years. I swear I don't know anything.'

Gryffin sends him to join his brother then pulls another sack from the pile, filling it with credits. Once he's bagged as much as he can find, he brings it into the back room. Kellyn has loaded most of the weapons so Gryffin goes to the back door and looks out. Something in the mound behind the hut catches his attention. Without speaking to Kellyn he steps outside and examines it. It takes him another minute to figure out what he's looking at. Clever bastards. He pushes his metal fingers into the seemingly random pile of scrap and finds a deep groove. A perfectly straight channel just below the first layer of rubbish. His fingers follow it as high as his six-foot-seven frame can reach. There must be something big in there. 'Kellyn! Brings their hands.'

As he waits, Gryffin pulls as much of the cover away from the structure as he can reach then stands back to get a proper look. Kellyn stops beside him carrying a bucket of hands. 'What the hell is that?'

Gryffin ignores him, taking a hand from the bucket and pressing it to the panel he uncovered. Nothing, He discards the hand over his shoulder and tries the next, getting a winner. He steps back beside Kellyn as the door opens. Both men look at each other and smile.

∞

Rayde checks the time again. Thirty minutes until the rendezvous with the transport. He readjusts his position in the command chair and sighs. He can't get comfortable. No matter what he tries, his thoughts continue to wander back to Gryffin and his first mission as leader of a team. A lot is riding on the outcome - for Gryffin and the Nomad as a whole. He checks the time again and curses to himself.

'Sir.'

'What is it?'

'Unknown ship heading our way. It's transmitting.'

'Ignore it.'

'No, sir. You don't understand. It's transmitting a Nomad code.'

'Kellyn's on that ship?'

'It's Gryffin's ID code.'

Rayde sits forward and stares at the signal on the long-range sensors. 'Let's see what he has to say.' Gryffin appears on the screen, looking very much alive and well. 'What's going on, son?'

'Ran into trouble. Permission to dock?'

Rayde pauses, examining the young man's face. He doesn't seem to be under duress. None of this is making sense. With no other option, he nods. 'Granted.' When the connection is cut, Rayde contacts a security team. If Gryffin has somehow been compromised or the damn thing in his head has malfunctioned, he wants a full team on standby.

23

The Arta's ship shudders as it docks with *Ares*. The vessel is roughly half the size of the Nomad ship but a few decades newer. Selling guns and selling out people was a lucrative business if this hi-tech ship is anything to go by.

Gryffin releases the controls and looks out the window along the side of *Ares*. Nerves don't usually affect him, but he's not racing to get off the ship. He let Rayde down on his very first mission. Rayde gave him orders and he screwed up every one of them. Yes, he got the guns and more credits than they came with, but he lost their original transport and his team came too close to being someone's property - something he knows about all too well. There's no telling how Rayde will take the news. There's a chance he could kick him off the crew. All he knows is the Nomad and *Ares*. If Rayde tells him to leave, he's got nowhere else to go. He'd be alone again.

'Sir?'

He doesn't bother turning to face Kellyn. 'What?'

'Rayde wants you to stay on board. He's sent a team to wait with you.'

Gryffin glances over his shoulder surprised at Kellyn's expression. The Nomad is angry. Probably at him for nearly getting them all killed. 'Get the men to the med bay. You too.'

Kellyn opens his mouth but shakes his head. 'Yes, sir.'

Gryffin gets out of the command chair. He stops in the centre of the deck, remaining motionless as the eight heavily armed Nomad take up position around him. A set of restraints is thrown at his feet. It's the set Rayde had made especially for him after he broke out of three pairs of standard restraints. Rayde must think he's compromised. His day is going from bad to fucking terrible. Resisting will get him a stun gun in the chest so he picks up the restraints and secures one side around his metal wrist. He holds his arms behind his back and, with a bit of manoeuvring, fixes the other side around his flesh wrist. Now all he can do is wait while Rayde gets the story from the rest of the team.

Rayde keeps him waiting for at least an hour –

maybe more. The only way Gryffin had to judge the time was by the actions of his security team. Their once firm stance has softened slightly while they stood guard around him. It was an uncomfortable wait for all of them. He's lost all feeling in his hand from the heavy restraints and his shoulders are killing him. Sheer stubbornness is the only thing keeping him from collapsing with exhaustion. Today's disaster helped destroy whatever reputation he had managed to scrape together. Landing on his ass in front of a security team would finish him off for good.

His eyes drift close for a few seconds before he jolts himself awake again. He adjusts his stance, locking his knees in an attempt to remain upright a little longer. A thick band of pain circles the end of his right arm. The combined weight of the restraints and the metal arm is fucking painful on his sensitive connectors. The arm needs to come off and, if he had a say, go on a one way trip out the airlock. Forget about food. All he wants right now is to submerge the remains of his arm in ice while he sleeps.

When Rayde finally makes an appearance, Gryffin is still standing but the headache has turned into a violent ball trying to escape through his eye sockets. Even blinking hurts like hell. Ignoring the pain, Gryffin keeps his eyes focused ahead of him as Rayde rests his hands on his hips, staring blankly at him, his heavily lined face completely unreadable. Gryffin frowns as Rayde suddenly slaps him on the shoulder, releasing a deep, booming laugh. 'What the hell have you done, son?'

'Sir?'

Rayde crosses his arms, still trying to stifle his rumbling laugh. 'I send you with credits to buy a few guns. So you come back with more credits, five times the amount of guns and this.' He holds his hands out and looks around the ship. 'That's pretty damn impressive.'

'I lost the transport. The team were captured by Slavers.'

'Oh, I know every tiny detail, son. I know you... how did Kellyn put it, appeared out of thin air and rammed your fist into the engine before single-handedly taking out each of the Slavers. Then you deal with the thieving Arta's. I have to say, that's a new Nomad record.'

'You're not angry?'

Rayde frowns as he unlocks the restraints from Gryffin's wrists. 'Angry? Why the devil would you think I'd be angry? True, it didn't quite go to plan, but you more than made up for that. Besides, missions rarely go to plan. If they did, we'd suffer no losses and be bathing in credits. Missions go bad. It's how we deal with them that matters. And you more than dealt with this. I apologise for the precautions. Having you appear in this impressive vessel raised a few alarms. You understand I had to be sure. Didn't want this to be some kind of booby trap. You probably won't give a damn, but you've managed to win over six of your biggest doubters. Your team collectively are singing your praises. You're their damn hero, son. Well done.'

Rayde walks around the command deck of the new ship. 'This is very nice. Why don't you get yourself checked out, grab a quick shower and some food? I want you in the training room in an hour.'

Gryffin restrains the groan. The last thing he needs or wants is to go anywhere near the training room. If he never sees the place again he'll die happy. 'Sir, I'm tired.'

'You think an enemy would let you off just because you missed a few hours in your bunk? I've told you what I want you to do. One hour, Gryffin.'

'Yes, sir.' Gryffin wills his body to move, leaving Rayde to explore his new toy.

24

Gryffin groans as an irritating buzzing wakes him. He buries his head under his pillow, but the sound penetrates the material. He throws the pillow to the end of his bed and glares over at the door. Rayde had kept him in the training room for three hours after he got back from his mission. He's only been back in his room half an hour. The captain can't want him so soon... can he?

Supressing a groan, he swings his legs off the cot and picks the ice pack from the floor where he dropped it when he fell asleep. He presses it to his stump, gritting his teeth as the cold penetrates the swollen flesh. 'Yeah.'

The door slides back and Kellyn stands in the entrance, his hands stuffed into the back pockets of his trousers. Of all the people to come calling, Kellyn wasn't on the list. He glances down at his holster before remembering he's always disarmed when he's on the ship. Too much of a risk leaving him with a weapon. He looks up at Kellyn but can't see any hostility on his face. 'What do you want?'

Kellyn's eyes lock on Gryffin's prosthetic lying on the floor beside his bed, then focuses on the icepack covered remains of his arm. 'You okay?'

'What do you want?' he repeats.

Kellyn looks down at his boots as he clears his throat. 'I came to apologise.'

Gryffin frowns, certain he misheard. 'You what?'

Kellyn lifts his head and smirks. 'Apologise. Yeah, it's not the done thing, I know. I reckon it's necessary in this case. I was a stubborn, ignorant, bull-headed idiot. I thought I knew better. I thought you'd, well, fuck up, to be honest.'

'I did.'

Kellyn laughs and shakes his head. 'If that's your idea of a fuck-up I can't wait to see what else you have planned. You saved all our necks. Necks that only needed saving thanks to me. I'm in your debt, Gryffin.' He drops his head again, focusing on his boots. 'And for what it's worth, I apologise for leading that ambush in the training room. Beating on you, it... fuck. It wasn't right.' He meets Gryffin's eyes and shrugs. 'I guess I should have trusted Rayde knew what he was doing when he made you a Nomad. I regret my part in what happened to you that day. Fuck all I can do about that now I know.'

Gryffin silently stares at Kellyn. First Rayde praises him for losing a transport and now the Nomad with the biggest issue about his place on the crew is apologising.

'Anyway, I told Rayde the way it went down today. He's left my punishment to you.' Kellyn holds his arms out to the side. 'So, I'll go with whatever you decide.'

Gryffin finally connects with his brain and places the icepack on the bed beside him. He gets up and faces one of the people who has made his life on *Ares* difficult. Kellyn's actions that day all those years ago had forced whatever is in Gryffin's head out of hiding. Maybe that's something he should be grateful for, but it's far from what he feels. If anything, he'd be quite happy to have left that part of himself undiscovered. If not for Kellyn's ambush he'd still be in blissful ignorance about how much the Scientist had fucked his body up.

Who's he kidding. It would have happened sooner or later. Kellyn just got there first.

Gryffin isn't an idiot. He knows what Rayde is expecting him to do. The captain is giving him the chance to get rid of this pain in his ass and face no backlash from the crew. Remembering the last time he was asked to do something like this, he looks down at the intricate griffin wing stretching across his chest.

It's a constant reminder of the Nomad life he took to get the mark of honour. There's no room on his body for another tattoo like that.

'I'm not going to punish you. Rayde's the captain. It's his place - not mine.'

Kellyn doesn't hide his shock. 'You sure? I deserve a hell of a kicking after what I did.'

'It's done.'

Kellyn nods. 'I appreciate that. You're a better Nomad than I've ever been.' He turns to leave and Gryffin lowers onto the edge of his bed, holding the icepack to his arm again. Kellyn stops and looks at him. 'I've put my name down for the next team you lead. Never had so much fun on a mission - well, apart from the nearly getting sold by Slavers bit. Hey, you sure you're okay? You need anything from the med bay?'

Gryffin shakes his head. 'No.'

Kellyn nods and walks away. Before he reaches the end of the corridor he turns around. 'A few more wins like that and you'll earn yourself a decent promotion. Maybe captain your own ship in a few years. Reckon you'll give the Nomad the shake-up we need.'

Gryffin looks after Kellyn long after he's gone. Captain? After what happened today, he's damn grateful to still have a place on the crew.

PART 9

1 YEAR LATER

GRYFFIN – 28 YEARS OLD
BRAY – 23 YEARS OLD

25

Bray wakes with a shout and sits up in bed. He rubs his eyes, looking around him, trying to figure out where the hell he is. 'Lights.'

He winces as the lights flick on, bathing the small room in light. It takes him another few seconds to realise where he is. He arrived on the colony a few hours ago and targeted one of its many bars. Since he had to part company with Hardy the well had well and truly run dry. The Foundation were tightening their grip on the border worlds, leaving him constantly dodging their ships. He was running low on provisions, fuel, and was worn out. The Foundation wasn't picky about who they were targeting. Keeping out of their reach was top of his list.

He lies back in bed and nearly screams as a hand moves across his bare chest, pulling him close. His companion is as naked as he is, and thankfully asleep. Probably should have taken it easy on the ale. He slips out from under her arm, whoever she is, gathers his clothes from various locations in the room, then slips into the cramped bathroom and gets dressed.

After checking she hasn't helped herself to credits from his wallet he creeps out of the room, gently closing the door behind him. Once outside, he pulls his hood up and tries to get his bearings. Whatever he was drinking last night did the job with his head. He can't remember anything after he got to the bar. He picks a path and starts walking. The priority is to get away from the room before his mystery guest wakes up.

Bray rounds the corner and skids to a stop. In the centre of the town, a team of security personnel are shoving locals into groups while others are bursting through doors, dragging people outside. He grabs a local hurrying past. 'Who are they?'

The man looks over his shoulder. 'Tyrat prison guards. They have dozens of warrants.' He pushes past Bray, disappearing down a side alley.

'Well that's not good,' Bray mutters to himself. Between his weapons trading and odd venture into other not so legal areas there's a fair chance he's on that warrant list. As Bray moves out a bit from the safety of the building, he gets a better view of the alleys leading into the square. Each of the four alleys is guarded.

He retreats the way he came. With no fucking clue where he is or where his transport is, he's fairly screwed. A wooden ladder hangs from the roof of the building opposite him. He pulls himself up onto the crates leaning against the back of the building and hauls himself onto the ladder then up to the roof. Luckily the men in the square are concentrating on the main paths instead of above them.

Bray crouches on the straw roof and runs to the edge, clearing the gap between the two buildings with ease. Three buildings later he silently lands on the roof of the main town hall. To make the most of the natural light, the building has large windows to either side of the peaked roof. He carefully peers into the nearest one and looks into the room below. He recognises most of the unlucky captives. From the looks of it, the prison guards are using the building to round up anyone with a record – including him.

He suppresses a curse when he spots the six bodies covered in cloth at the side of the room. They don't care if they bring them back cold or warm. This is getting out of hand. He needs to get off this planet - now.

Bray flattens his body to the roof as gunfire sounds in the distance. That's his cue to move. The adrenaline rushes around his body as he gets up. Crouching, he hurries across the roof to the tall chimney sprouting out of the top of the adjoining wall. He's fucked unless he finds his transport - ideally before the Foundation does.

He climbs up the tall stack, keeping his body out of sight of the town square. 'C'mon, where the hell did I put you?' The prison transports are easy to spot. Doesn't help they're at the entrance to the large open area where his transport is sitting. He winces as the headache he woke up with kicks back in. Tackling a prison ground crew while hungover doesn't give him the best odds at coming out of this in one piece.

He leaves the safety of the chimney stack and slides on his belly towards the back of the roof. He holds his breath as he lands on the gravel path, but no one seems to have heard him. He hurries across town and scales the fence leading to the landing area. His ship is a short sprint across the yard. He checks for any unwanted spectators then ducks low as he clears the ground. He presses himself against the side of his ship and waits. Nothing. No shouts or footsteps heading in his direction. He keys the code into the door. The grinding of gears echoes as the door slides aside. He was meant to see to that last week. Serves him right if it bites him in the ass now.

Bray rounds the corner, his gun raised. He lowers the weapon and blows out a breath. The cockpit is empty. He throws himself at the seat, flicking the ignition switches, praying the temperamental craft obeys without the usual kicking and thumping. Something hard and cold presses against the back of his head. 'Hands up.'

Bray tightens the grip on the lever. 'Fine. Just don't shoot.'

The gun pushes against his scalp. 'Hands up or I will shoot.'

Bray releases the control and raises his hands. He can see the man in the reflection in front of him. When the man moves to get the restraints from his belt, Bray shoves the knife hidden in his sleeve into the man's leg. He screams and backs away giving Bray space to get up and thump him in the face with the hilt of his knife, knocking him out.

He gets back in his seat and starts the ignition. 'Guess you're coming for a ride, buddy.'

'Think you'll be coming for a ride with us, buddy.'

He looks over his shoulder to find another man standing over the body. 'Give me a fucking break.'

He flashes an ID badge at Bray. 'I'm from Tyrat Prison Moon. Quite a hefty load on your head, Brayden Liam Sawyer. And we're going to collect.'

Bray smirks and throws the ship into its launch sequence. Her antique engines manage to lift her off the ground in her usual way - sideways. The man crashes into the wall but quickly regains his footing. Bray sends the ship higher. The guard fires at him, narrowly missing his head and the controls.

Bray leaves the ship on autopilot and launches himself at the guard. Instead of firing and taking his ship down, Bray hammers the butt of his weapon against the man's shoulder. The man drops his gun, but instead of backing off, he lunges at Bray. His uninjured shoulder ploughs into Bray's chest, driving the air from his lungs. His back slams against the wall, his head hitting the corner of the panel above him. He shakes the stars from his vision as he grabs the man's head and drives his knee into his face. The guard drops to the floor clutching his face, blood pouring from between his fingers.

Alarms scream to life. Something has targeted his ship. He tries to get back to his seat but his new friend isn't too keen. He grabs Bray's ankle slamming him to the ground. He flips onto this back and kicks out with his other foot, but the bastard keeps dodging.

The intensity of the alarms increases and the ship jolts violently again and again. He looks back at the man, smearing his blood over Bray's leg. 'Fuck off!' He kicks out again and this time he hits the guy's already smashed nose. He lets go long enough for Bray to scramble to his feet and jump into the cockpit.

He doesn't need to check the monitors to see just what level of shit he's in. The Tyrat transport is in front of his transport. Two heavy tethers link the ship and he's being reeled to the ground like a damn fish. Just when he thinks things couldn't get worse, another missile hits, killing his remaining engine. Looks like they don't want him to have a soft landing.

His ship hangs for what feels like a long time before it drops like a stone. Bray hurries to fasten his harness, getting the buckle clipped as the ship slams into the ground.

26

UNINHABITED MOON

Rayde leans against the side of the transport and takes in the sight in front of him. To the right, *Ares* sits in the sand, her large sails open as Nomad work on long-overdue repairs. To the left, slightly smaller but no less impressive, his new ship. The Arta brothers' kind donation to the cause had been renamed *Kratos*, and from tomorrow, it'll be his new home.

He swallows but the bitter taste remains in his mouth. For the best part of twenty years, he'd captained *Ares*. No longer. The crew had spoken and he could do nothing about it. *Ares* now belongs to Gryffin. It's not a move he's in any way happy about but it's difficult to argue with the facts – or a ship full of Nomad all backing Gryffin. Since that fateful day when he sent his protege to buy guns from the Arta Brothers, things had shifted within the crew. Those who had originally been less than thrilled with the prospect of sharing their space with a cyborg, or whatever the hell the boy is, had altered their way of thinking. And could he blame them?

He glares at the six Nomad working on the stern of his... Gryffin's ship. They had painted over his symbol, replacing the dagger with a griffin. The fierce creature matches the tattoo on Gryffin's body. He takes a sip from his flask as the man responsible for his unplanned relocation appears.

Gryffin strides towards him and at that moment, Rayde realises the difference in the boy since that first mission. With an impressive array of weapons hanging from holsters on his hip and leg, Gryffin certainly looks like someone you wouldn't want to get on the wrong side of. Constant training and three meals a day had transformed the half-dead corpse he had tripped over all those years ago into a formidable Nomad. His shoulders are back, his strides long, his eyes constantly moving, taking in every detail of his surroundings. He's strong, confident and more than capable of killing everyone here without breaking into a sweat. He's everything Rayde wanted him to be. Everything Rayde trained him to be. A cold, calculated, lethal fighter. Someone to bring people to their knees in the presence of the Nomad. The problem is, he was meant to bring people to their knees in front of Rayde. He was meant to solidify Rayde's hold on the Nomad. He was meant to be Rayde's iron fist not steal his fucking ship from under him.

Rayde takes another drink from his flask. It's only a matter of time before he takes command of the boy again. He's sure of it. Gryffin better not get too comfortable in the captain's chair. It's only a matter of time before *Ares* and *Kratos* would fly together under his colours again.

Rayde forces a smile on his face as Gryffin stops beside him. 'How do you feel, Captain?'

Gryffin glances at him but doesn't reply.

'Problem, son?'

'This isn't right, sir.'

'You don't like the griffin?'

'Not that. Getting *Ares*.'

No arguments from him on that point. 'You don't want her? She not good enough for you?'

Gryffin frowns at him, that confidence weakening a little when he thinks he's got on Rayde's wrong side. That's good to see. At least he still has a hold over the boy. 'She's yours, sir.'

'I love that ship, but it's time I pass her on. Besides, that new ship you... acquired, has a lot going for it. Can't say I'm not looking forward to having a ship that doesn't fall apart when you look at it.' He laughs and shakes his head. '*Ares* is a young man's ship, son. I'm not that young man anymore. She'll keep you on your toes.'

Gryffin nods but looks far from convinced.

'You look through the list of the crew I recommended. You pick a second in command yet?'

'Sayber.'

'Good choice. He would have been my choice too. I've taken a skeleton crew to keep *Kratos* running until I can recruit. We're a few days from the nearest station. No doubt I'll find a few willing bodies there. The Nomad are earning quite a reputation thanks to your antics off the ship. Your no-nonsense way of doing things is working wonders for us.' Rayde glances at the young man. He's staring over at *Ares*, his arms folded and his expression stern. 'You need to keep that up, you know that, right.'

Gryffin nods. 'Just want the best for the Nomad.'

'No one would argue about that. You've taken a path and you must stick to it. You've progressed more than I thought you would. The Nomad have a place in the Sector again. A serious place. That's thanks to you. I must have heard from a dozen other Captains since I set you lose. They've all heard about what you did - what you're doing. Most heard about it from other sources. You're making a name for the Nomad. Keep it up, you get me?'

Gryffin nods again.

'Okay then. Well, I'm going to pack up the rest of my things. Time to make myself at home on *Kratos*. Just one word of advice, Captain.'

Gryffin looks at him, his ocular implant barely visible through his long hair. Something Rayde would prefer he has a rethink about. Those implants would serve the Nomad best if they were on show. 'Might be best you work on saying a little more every now and again. You'll need to give your crew the odd order.'

'Yes, sir.'

Rayde shakes his head as he walks back to *Kratos*. Gryffin's crew are in for an interesting time. Serves them right.

27

TYRAT PRISON MOON

'Name.'

Bray spits out blood and rubs his aching jaw. 'You know my name so why ask?'

The prison guard glares at him over this handheld. 'Because I like when you refuse and we get to do this.'

His mate strikes Bray across the face with the end of his baton. At least he hasn't powered up the shock stick. Much more fun to use the blunt end. 'Fine. Bray.'

'Full name. You were born on Earth weren't you.'

'Brayden Liam Sawyer. The First.' That earns him another strike. Probably best he keeps his mouth shut.

'As a Foundation resident, you are entitled to

contact your family.'

'I'll pass.'

'Suit yourself. Mark him then straight to Gen Pop.'

Bray's shackled feet struggle to keep up with the guard as he's led through the dark tunnels from intake to a room Bray guesses is used as a med bay. Not that you'd want to come here with anything medical related. It would be a one way visit. The stench of rot hangs thick in the air which explains the masks the guards wear.

A heavyset woman slips on a pair of gloves as Bray is thrown face down on a metal table. The guards add their weight to his back as the woman roughly pushes his sleeve up and holds a metal plate against his upper left arm. He hisses as what feels like a thousand needles pierce his flesh. She pulls it away and leans down to examine her work. Satisfied, they unlock him and push him off the table while she prepares for the next inmate. Bray looks down at his arm. They've put his initials and a series of numbers on him. BS-4-31. Great. So now he's got BS tattooed on his arm. That's going to make him a human punching bag.

They drag him to another room and unlock the restraints. A pile of black prison uniforms is on the metal bench against the far wall. It's the black pool of liquid in front of him he's not sure about. He's told to strip and then his hands are chained again. The guards loop the chain through a heavy hook above him and he is lifted off the ground. Before he can react, he is dropped into the freezing liquid. He thrashes in the dark but after a few seconds, he is lifted out and dumped on the ground. The heavy smell of disinfectant replaces the rot. He dresses quickly and lines up against the far wall as three other men are dunked behind him. Once everyone is in place, the floor withdraws dropping the inmates into the main prison below. Bray lands on the hard ground and quickly rolls out of the way before anyone else lands on him. He looks around and the fear he was trying to keep at bay rises to the surface. Dozens of inmates gather around the newcomers, eyeing each of the men like a predator would a fresh piece of meat.

'In your cells!'

The shout echoes through the speakers, stopping whatever was about to happen. With barely contained contempt, the inmates shuffle away to their cells. Bray looks around, unsure of what to do or where to go.

'Hey. New meat.' He looks above him and sees a guard standing on a metal walkway suspended above him. 'Cell number is on your arm. Move!'

Bray ignores the other new inmates and finds the codes written on the wall beside him. He's in section 4 cell 31. Moving with more confidence than he feels, he finds the correct area and stands at the door to his cell. At least he doesn't have to share with anyone. Well, except for whatever the hell that thing is crawling up the wall. The mutated cockroach carries on with its business as Bray steps inside. The door slides shut behind him, trapping him in the tiny cell with his new multiple legged friend.

He jumps as a metal bowl is slid through the bars. The pale brown mass must be the substitute for a meat substitute. He can smell it from here and he'd rather eat the cockroach. He considers the bread for a second longer. Whatever is growing up the side of it would excite most scientists. Looks like he'll be going hungry.

He sits on the bed, causing a wave of stale urine to waft up and add to the other odours in this place. He shuffles back against the wall, keeping an eye on the roach as he wraps his arms around his legs.

If only his family could see him now. He's only gone and proved them right. He fucked up one too many times and now look at him. When he left Vana he wanted to make a life for himself. But every single step, every turn he took was wrong. He went from mistake to mistake and instead of proving himself, he's in here for the rest of his life. He buries his head in his knees and wills the tears away, but they keep coming.

28

TRADERS MARKET

Gryffin stops in front of the trader and examines the weapons laid out on the table.

Rafe pops a nut of some sort into his mouth and smiles as he chews loudly. 'Best out there. You're getting them for a steal.' Rafe snorts as he laughs at his own joke. If he didn't need to deal with Rafe again he'd happily put a bullet in his nut-filled mouth.

'Usual price.'

Rafe makes a face as he swallows. 'Not sure that'll work for me. Like I said, these are the best out there.' He reaches for another nut but Gryffin pulls the bowl out of his reach.

'Usual price or I walk.'

'I'd love to help you but I can't just give them away.' Gryffin turns towards the door. 'Wait! Fine. Usual price. You're going to bankrupt me at this rate.'

Gryffin takes the bag from Kellyn and hands over the credits. 'Pack the guns.'

Rafe takes two glasses from the cupboard under his desk and places them beside a bottle of purple liquid. 'Why the rush? Stop for a bit and have a drink.'

The Nomad team gather the guns and load them into three heavy bags on the floor.

'C'mon, Captain. Have a drink with me. Please.'

The please followed by the glance at his wrist unit sends alarm bells off in Gryffin's head. 'Time to go.'

Ignoring Rafe's protests, Gryffin and his team leave the room, hands on weapons and fully expecting trouble. Nothing seems off as they enter the alley outside. Sayber contacts him before he gets the chance to activate his comms.

'What is it?'

'Prison guards from Tyrat. Three ships.'

'Thought something was up. How long?'

'They've already landed.'

'What the hell do you mean?'

'I've been trying to get in contact for a while. Comms must have been blocked. You done with Rafe?'

'Just finished. Must have had something in his shop to block comms. He was acting off at the end. Wanted us to stay longer.'

'Bastard must have a hand in this. Best you get out

of there. Now.'

'Get *Ares* away from here and cloaked. We'll head back to the transport.'

'Keep comms open. I'll track you from here.'

He pulls his hood down, hiding his face a little more. If they're to make it back to the transport he needs to find another way. Through the town would be asking for trouble. He checks the map on his unit and realises they're screwed. The only way back is through the village or at least skirting the edge of it. Thanks to the mountains surrounding them, any other option is out unless they fancied a three-day hike.

They reach the town and are met with hundreds of traders. Their stalls, carts and shop-fronts are laden with goods from all across the Sector. Market day. The crowd will slow them down but should help mask them. Gryffin slowly scans the crowd. It takes a few minutes but he picks out the guards, the restraints and shock sticks they carry under their jackets adding to their bulk. They also help make them slower, more awkward if engaged in combat.

'Sir?'

'Bit busy, Sayber.'

'I've just intercepted a message. They're after you. It's not much of a description, but they're hunting for the Captain of *Ares*. Rough height, hair colour, metal on your face.'

'What?'

'Sounds like someone got a look at you at some stage. You better move your arse.'

He turns to his team. 'Split up. We move through there as one, we'll be picked off.'

One by one, the Nomad team merge with the locals, picking their way through the throng. The hairs on the back of Gryffin's neck prickle. He keeps his hand on his gun, but that offers little comfort. Something feels wrong about this. He looks left and right, seeing the rest of the Nomad making slow but steady progress. 'Kellyn, you got one dead ahead.' Kellyn discretely pauses at a stall, moving behind a stand of furs as the guard continues past him. Usually, he'd take pleasure taking every one of them down, but the market is too full of innocent travellers and locals. It would be a slaughter - one he'd prefer to keep the Nomad name far away from.

He's got roughly halfway through when the heavy murmur of conversation dies away. Shopkeepers and traders alike fall silent.

He hisses into his comms. 'Stop. Now.'

'We're looking for a Nomad.'

Along with everyone else, Gryffin lifts his head to look at the man standing on top of the well in the centre of the square. He holds up a set of restraints. 'Just want him. I know there's a bit of loyalty to the Nomad. Take a look around. Is that loyalty worth lives? My men have hostages. They live if this Nomad comes with us.'

Gryffin sees at least two dozen men through the square, a weapon pressed against the heads of women, men and children. 'We take him or we hurt these nice people. Your choice.'

The guard barely waits long enough for a response before he fires. One of the men held hostage crumples to the ground surrounded by a chorus of screams. The villager writhes on the ground, blood oozing from the wound on his leg. 'Where are you? Perhaps I didn't make myself clear. You or all of them. Time's getting on, Captain.'

'Don't you fucking move,' Sayber mutters into his ear. 'You give yourself up, they'll kill everyone anyway. Bounty's too high to give a damn about them.'

Gryffin glances to the side. An old motorbike is propped up against the wall behind the stall. If he can get to it he can lure the men away from the locals. He ducks behind the stall and mounts the bike. The machine is so old it is key-operated, but that suits him fine - especially when the key is hanging from the handlebar. He slips it into the port and presses his thumb against the ignition. With a roar, the bike comes to life. Over the sound of the engine, he can hear shouting from the market. 'I'll lead them away. Get the rest of the crew off the surface.'

He ignores anything else Sayber may have said as he moves through the town, scattering locals like leaves as he passes. He checks over his shoulder and smiles to himself when he sees the men getting into a transport and following him. He kicks the bike up a gear and takes the road into the mountains bordering the town. Once out of the populated area, he'll take these bastards down.

It may be old, but the bike is faster than the transport on this terrain so he slows down a little. He doesn't want them to lose him and have them fall back to the town. He rounds the corner and comes to a stop across the road. He lifts his gun and waits for the first transport to approach. The driver is dead before the transport has completed the turn. The passenger ducks, avoiding the round with his name on it. Gryffin moves the bike out of the way as the transport veers off the road and crashes into the trees, coming to a stop on its side.

He abandons the bike and climbs on top of the transport. He rams his metal fingers into the gap at the side of the door and pulls back. After a brief fight, the hatch gives way, creaking open. He fires through the opening, taking out the four occupants.

The second transport slows as it approaches the wreckage. Gryffin targets the driver, but he veers the transport to the side, avoiding the round. It crashes off the road, taking down a few trees as it ploughs a path for itself. The driver manages to keep it steady, bringing it back on the road ahead of the crashed vehicle. Gryffin leaps off the top of the transport, ploughs through the undergrowth to the bike, and takes off after the second vehicle. He catches up with it less than a minute later. He pulls hard on the brakes, sending the bike skidding out from under him. Bike and rider tear across the dirt road, stones and debris leaving their mark on both until they come to a stop. Gryffin shoves the bike off his leg and looks at the group facing him, blocking the road. There must be at least thirty guards slowly encircling him. The bastards share the same victorious smile as they move closer to each other, forming a tight barrier.

The head guard from the town steps out from behind the others. He stands in front of Gryffin with his hands on his hips. 'You killed my men.'

'Payback for hurting the local.'

'One market rat does not equal five guards. Who knows, the bounty may increase after that. These fine gentlemen could have a large cut thanks to your actions here today. Kindly remove his weapons. Wouldn't want him doing something he shouldn't.'

Three men approach him from behind, two keeping their weapons on the back of his head while the third reaches down to pull his gun out of its holster. His knife follows next. They don't bother searching for any more weapons. Not a lot he could do anyway with this number of targets.

The guard pulls a thick baton from his belt and crouches down in front of Gryffin. 'Prison-grade shock stick. Quite a powerful punch. I've been told it's like being hit by a transport.'

Gryffin's first instinct is to use the control implant to help get him out of this mess but reins himself in. The guards may or may not know what he is. The last thing he wants to do is show them what he can do - especially since the odds of him getting out are non-existent. Even with the control implant, he can't take down this many without doing himself some serious damage.

He had to give it to the guard, it is like being hit with a transport. He gasps, his lungs struggling to get back in sync with his implants. Gryffin looks back at the guard and braces for another blast. By the time the transport has pulled up beside him, Gryffin and the stick have been up close and personal eight times. His muscles have turned to jelly which is fine because his bones feel too heavy for his body. He's stuck on the ground in an uncooperative body as the guards restrain him and drag him into the waiting transport.

29

Rafe stops in front of the heavy steel doors, his arms crossed over his chest. 'I'm sorry about this, Captain. It's just business.'

Gryffin doesn't respond - just raises his eyebrow as he looks at his former trading partner. Rafe was the reason he was there in the first place. Seems the bounty was more enticing than regular income from the Nomad.

'Don't give me that look. I've seen you give people that look. Doesn't go well for them. I had no choice, okay. The bounty had been doubled. Doubled! And they were threatening my business. Said they'd raze the place to the ground if I didn't lure you in.'

'What do you think I'm going to do to you?'

Rafe laughs nervously. 'Well, the way I see it, you're in there. As long as they're pointing their guns at you, you're not pointing your gun at me. Figure I'm pretty safe.'

Gryffin rises to his feet, the heavy chains securing him to the floor creaking as he pulls against them. 'That what you figure?'

Rafe pauses as he intently examines the chains holding Gryffin back. 'Never seen someone take eight hits from the stick before. How the hell did you stay upright so long? I was watching from the transport. It was hurting but you kept going back for more. How?'

Gryffin keeps his gaze steady as the man flaps under the scrutiny.

'Yeah, probably not the right time. Bigger things on your mind. Don't know if you heard but you're going to Tyrat. At last I didn't sell you out to the Slavers. They're offering a bounty too. Not as much though. No resale value for them. Slavers don't want to risk retraining you to sell you. Apparently, no one would want to own something that could kill them.' He laughs and scratches the back of his neck. 'But that's better for you, right? I mean at least you won't have a master.'

The conversation is cut short when a team of prison guards step into the room. Gryffin keeps eye contact with Rafe as his list of charges is read out loud. He isn't asked to confirm or deny. Tyrat isn't about that. If they get you, you're considered guilty - whether you are or not. He falls into the first category.

The cell is opened and two men approach him. They unlock his ankles and wrists from the floor, attaching them to heavy metal rods they can lead him on. Before they can adjust their grip on the seemingly placid prisoner, Gryffin slams his elbow into the neck of the nearest guard. The man falls soundlessly to the ground. Gryffin swings the chain connecting his hands to the rod, using it as a pendulum. The second guard falls when the rod strikes the side of his head with a wet thud.

Gryffin grabs Rafe by the collar of his shirt. He smacks his head against Rafe's nose, shattering the bone. Rafe clutches his face. His screams are drowned out as another team crashes into the cell. Three of the guards take aim and small projectiles attach to him. Whatever drug they're loaded with works into his system. It'll take time for his implants to neutralise whatever it is. His muscles weaken and a heavy fog settles over him. Whatever the guards say is lost in the fog. He wants to retaliate, to fight back but he can't get the commands to the rest of his body. One of the guards approaches him with a heavy hood in his hands. He pulls it over Gryffin's head and his world goes black.

∞

'Well, well, well. Not so tough now, are you, scum?'

The three men laugh as they walk around Gryffin. He stands still, not trying to get out of his restraints. Whatever they shot him up with has left his brain and body not on speaking terms. His implants are struggling to clear the drug from his system. He's just going to have to sit this out until he's back to full strength again.

One of the men rams him in the side with a shock stick. Gryffin grunts as it releases a charge into him. He doubles over, gasping for breath when the guard finally breaks contact. The same man knocks him to the ground and takes out a large knife. Before he can struggle to his feet again, his jacket and top have been cut off, exposing his chest implant and arm. The men stop laughing and stare at him. He tries to get up but his damn legs still have a mind of their own.

'What the hell is that? Some sort of armour?'

'Looks like it's part of him.' He pokes Gryffin's chest implant with his stick. 'Wonder what it does.'

'How about we find out? Bounty doesn't detail the condition he's to be in.'

The guards don respirators before fixing another set of restraints, pinning his arms to his body. The lead guard shoves a gun against Gryffin's head. 'Walk.'

'Or what? Bounty's no good if I'm dead.'

'True, but the more you piss us off here, the worse it'll be for you later. Now get up and move your damn feet.'

Faced with staying here and being beaten he decides to go with them... and be beaten. If he's going to get out he needs to know his way around. Only one way to do that.

Gryffin's heard tales of this place, but as no one escaped he's not sure where those details came from. For a state of the art Foundation prison, he's not impressed so far. They haul him down a maze of corridors, each one darker and narrower than the one before. No polished steel walls. Seems they utilised the structure of the moon, fitting doors and cells into the rock. After less than a minute he realises why the guards wear respirators.

The air is warm and thick with the scent of human waste, sweat, decomp, and blood. The warm concoction coats his nostrils and creeps into his mouth, the taste turning his stomach.

His eyes blur in and out of focus and more than once he doesn't see a wall or a low ceiling in time. He's going to be a bloody mess by the time they get him wherever he's going.

The cramped tunnels open out into a monstrous cavern, lined with dozens of levels, each one housing hundreds of inmates in row after row of cages. Below him, men and women scream and chant as two inmates circle each other in a makeshift ring of spiked wire and feral prisoners. A few curious faces turn in his direction, but he doesn't hold their attention long. They've got more important things on their minds.

'Mark him?'

The lead guard shakes his head. 'I want to have some fun with him first.'

'Crate?'

'Why not. Give him a bit of downtime.' They pull him into a narrow room at the end of the corridor. Instead of cells the wall is lined with metal doors like those you'd find in a morgue. They open the nearest one and point towards it. 'In.'

Gryffin raises an eyebrow. That may be where he's going but it won't be without a fight.

A second dose of shock stick to his stomach sends him heading in the right direction. A severe shove from behind finishes the job. Instinct kicks in as they try to push him inside. He uses every last bit of his dwindling energy to fight back, but he's wasting his time. They don't even bother to uncuff him as they force him head first into the crate. Stars dance in his vision as his head hits the stone floor.

They slam the door shut, plunging him into darkness. He shuffles around, but his six-foot-seven frame isn't liking the four-foot-cube. The cage the Scientist kept him in was more spacious. He allows the control implant in his head a little freedom. If he freaks out in here, he's going to make things a hell of lot worse.

A click sounds from the front of the box and a fan whizzes to life. Repugnant, warm air fills the box adding to the rising panic he's trying to hold back. Something with a lot of legs scuttles over his hand, moving up his arm. He presses against the wall, hearing a satisfying crunch as his cellmate disintegrates.

30

Bray spits out a mouthful of blood and wipes his split lip. His opponent raises his arms and roars in victory, playing up to the watching hoard. Bray gets to his knees and groans as a broken rib protests. He glares at the prison guards watching from the gantry suspended over the communal area. Instead of trying to break up the fight, he sees credits exchange hands. No doubt they're betting on the other man. His opponent has never lost a fight so the odds are stacked against him.

That doesn't mean Bray's going to lie down and let himself get beaten to death. Bray forces himself to his feet and faces the other man. The crowd erupts again, smelling the blood about to be shed. As well as wanting the victory, and to keep his life, Bray needs the food the winner will get. The guards are less than generous when it comes to feeding the inmates. Anything to do with inmate well-being comes a distant second to betting on the fights. Being so far from the main Foundation territory, no one controls what the guards do... or don't do. Bray hasn't eaten for three days. If he has to kill this man for a meal, he'll do it.

The man growls and charges towards Bray. He braces for the impact. The two men collide, driving Bray's knee into the other man's groin. The man screams in pain and drops to the ground, doubled over. Bray hobbles over to him and kicks him in the kidneys. When the man arches back, Bray's boot makes contact with his already badly broken nose. With blood pouring down his face, the prisoner curses loudly at Bray as he struggles to get to his feet. The crowd screams for Bray to finish, and he's not going to disappoint. He drives his foot into the man's face, over and over. The muscles in his leg ache from the exertion, but something has taken over. He's not going to back down. He can't back down. Blood sprays on to his already splattered trousers as he ploughs his boot into the man's face for the final time. His opponent stops thrashing and his gargled screams stop. Bray falls to his knees beside the body and stares at the mess. The horror of what he's just done doesn't affect him. It probably should, but he's gone beyond caring.

He dismisses the body and looks up at the guards above him. 'Where's my food?'

One of the guards, a tall, thin man with greasy black hair and bad skin leans over the railing and nods once at his colleagues. Bray flinches as strong hands shove him to the ground. He lands hard on the dirty, blood-soaked stone, knocking the air from his lungs. Cold metal restraints lock around his wrists, biting into his skin. 'I want my fucking food!'

His demand is ignored as one of the guards shoves his knee into Bray's back, holding him down. Bray's not an idiot. He knows full well he's going to a cell and not to dinner. He bends his leg, kicking the guard in the back. The satisfaction of the blow is short-lived as the guard retaliates with a strike between his shoulder blades with his weapon.

They haul him to his feet and Bray glowers up at the greasy-haired man. 'I want fucking food!' Bray roars.

The guard stuffs a handful of credits into his pocket as he smiles down at Bray. 'Of course. I did promise.' He addresses the guards restraining Bray. 'Settle him in and make sure you feed him.' The snicker of laughter that follows him from the room doesn't fill him with much confidence. The crowd surges to life as he's led away. From what chanting and shouting he can hear, it seems he's their new favourite fighter. Just what he needs.

He tries to keep up with the guards but ends up letting them pull him along the corridor. His aching legs drag behind him, every bump sending waves of pain up his abused muscles. They open the heavy door to the sensory deprivation area and unlock one of the cells or "crates" as they are affectionately known. After receiving a sharp knee to the gut, Bray is helped head first into the box and the door is slammed shut.

31

Gryffin lies on his side in the dark, his knees drawn up to his chest in the cramped box. He'd lost feeling in both arms a while ago and his connectors in his prosthetic arm are aching. He could manoeuvre to lie on the other side, but he doesn't want to move. He's keeping himself curled up tight. That way he can't feel the walls pressing against him. He's keeping his eyes closed. That way he can't see the confines of the cramped cell. He's never been good in small spaces but never thought about it much. He's never had to stay somewhere so small for so long, completely helpless to do anything but scream. If he didn't force himself to stay still, he could easily let the panic take over. He'd take the operating table any day over this.

The fan splutters, dies then whirs back to life again. Gryffin tries to bury his nose in his knees, but the smell of decomp won't be masked. It clings to his tongue and coats his mouth. He squeezes his eyes shut as memories of his childhood join in the fun. To escape being dragged into his past, he opens his eyes but sees lines of cages with grotesque bodies still sealed inside. He looks up at the Scientist, a serene smile on his face as he hums to himself. Heavy restraints keep Gryffin in place, keeping his head turned to the side with a perfect view of the cages. The whine of the drill drowns out the Scientist's humming.

Gryffin shouts and slams his head against the top of the crate as he fights to get out. He kicks out, hitting the door. Or is it the wall? Completely disorientated the panic takes hold of him. Even with his night vision, all the walls look the same. He braces his feet against the wall as a wave of dizziness hits him, spinning the box. His lungs struggle to pull air into his body. Nausea twists his stomach as the foul-tasting air makes him retch. As fast as the suffocating panic hits, a quiet calm settles over his body. He knows his implants are stabilising him and for the first time in his life he couldn't be more grateful. He still feels sick and dizzy but the panic is subsiding as his heart rate and breathing steady.

He welcomes the numbness the implant brings. With his eyes closed again he concentrates on the steady beat of the fan. He doesn't know how long he zones out for, but his peace is suddenly disturbed by shouting and banging from outside his crate.

The shouting intensifies and Gryffin pushes to his elbow as someone kicks the door to his box. He hears the door next to his open and the prisoner gets the same help inside he did.

'I want my fucking food!'

The door slams and the prisoner loses control, shouting and cursing as the guards walk away. Poor fucker keeps up the screaming for another few minutes and Gryffin has a hard time not joining in. He squeezes his eyes shut as the other prisoner retches repeatedly. Doesn't say much about the food.

Gryffin quietens his breathing as a loud grinding sound comes from the top of the box near the hole where the fan is located. Freezing water pours into the box, quickly covering his base. It continues to rise, the icy water soaking into his clothes and chilling his skin. Gryffin tries to keep his face above water, taking a large lungful of air in case the water doesn't stop. Just before it hits the roof, the pump shuts down and the fan kicks into life again. If he presses his face against the roof there's just enough of a gap to take a foul smelling breath.

The confines of the box makes keeping his nose above the water a painful and tiring exercise. Muscles scream for relief and after a while he gives in, takes a deep breath and rests his head on the bottom. He lasts a few minutes thanks to his implants but needs to resurface to breathe again. The pain, the claustrophobia, it all disappears as he focuses on the basic task of keeping air in his lungs. He presses his nose to the roof as long as he can before lying back on the bottom, then repeats the whole process again. And again. And again.

32

Bray screams again and kicks the door, desperate to be let out of the crate. He curses loudly as the metal plate clatters at his feet. There goes his dinner. He gasps for breath, using up the little air he has. He roars, thrashing in the dark, trying to release his arms, but there's no way out. The ventilation system kicks in, pumping rancid, warm air into his crate.

Bray takes in a large lungful of the pungent air. His lungs are happy about the air, but his stomach and brain can't handle the stench. He retches until nothing else comes up, then stops struggling. A strange stillness takes over as he lies in the dark. He closes his eyes even though he can't see anything. At least with his eyes closed, he can pretend he's in his dark cell.

This is his third stint in the crate and he still hasn't got used to it. If anything, the claustrophobia gets worse with each spell in the box. He's only got himself to blame. If he'd just kept his mouth shut and stayed away from trouble, he'd be back in his cell right now. Why the hell does he have to keep sabotaging things for himself? His fucking self-destruct switch is permanently set to on and he can't do a thing about it.

He hears someone moving in the crate next to him but doesn't bother engaging in chit-chat. Fuck all to talk about and even less interest. It's probably the tall guy he saw being led in while he was fighting. Newbies were usually taken straight to the crate. The last thing he wants to hear about right now is life outside Tyrat. The only way to survive in here is to forget about all that. You'd drive yourself crazy otherwise.

His empty stomach growls reminding him his prize is somewhere in the dark with him. Even though he's not interested in eating, it might be the last food he sees for a while. And he fought damn hard for it - he's not about to let it go to waste.

He shuffles around the cell until his nose finds the food. Even with the stench from the ventilation area, the smell of the food is hard to miss. He doesn't know which smells worse. Whatever was on the plate is well and truly past its best. He's just glad he can't see what it is. Even though it's demanding food, his stomach shares his revulsion. Unfortunately, he either eats it or he goes hungry. Knowing the guards, they'll only leave the food with him for a short time.

He props himself up on an elbow, the movement digging the metal cuffs deep into his skin. Bray leans over, his nose hovering just above the food, and breathes through his mouth. Without thinking about what he's eating, he lowers his face into the mess. His nose pushes deep into the rancid food as he eats as much as he can as quick as he can. Two mouthfuls later and he's done. He rolls away from the food, pushing the plate to the bottom of the crate with his foot. He lies on his back, breathing through his mouth. The slop is coating his nose, and with his hands cuffed, it's going to have to stay there.

Bray concentrates on breathing, counting his breaths in and out, through his mouth. It may not have been a four-course meal but if he had to do it over, he'd still kill the other man to get it.

33

Gryffin fights back as someone grabs his ankle, wrenching him from the crate. He lands on the ground and takes deep breaths of better quality air. Not a whole lot better but anything is an improvement on whatever they pump into the crate. He lost track of how long he had been submerged for, but it was long enough. When the water drained away he was left in a soggy, freezing heap on the bottom of the box. For the next few hours, the sole purpose of the fan seemed to be pumping icy air into the crate. His implants had tried to regulate his body, tried to keep him warm, but they too had given up and called it quits. Every bone, every muscle aches from violent shivering. He's just damn lucky he didn't break a bone.

A boot to his ribs sends him to the ground where an indeterminate amount of bodies pile on top of him. Heavy chains are attached to his restraints and his ankles are shackled to each other with a short chain. 'Get up.'

He blinks and looks up at the same guard he met when he first arrived.

'I said get up. Or would you prefer to go back in the crate? Maybe this time we'll fill it with hot water. Boil you alive in there. Your choice.'

Even though his muscles ache from the cramped space, he convinces them to help him get up. He sways a little but manages to stay upright.

'Good boy. Now walk.' He points out the door with his baton. 'That way.'

Easier said than done thanks to the shackles. Each step is pathetic and uses far too much energy. Before he leaves the room holding the crates he glances over his shoulder. Another guard opens the cell next to his, slides a bowl of water in then slams the door shut. Gryffin shuffles away as the prisoner screams to be let out.

They lead him down a line of empty cells and open the last door. Two of the men hold him up while the third locks his wrists into the chains hanging on the back wall of the cell. Once he's finished, he chains Gryffin ankles to the floor then adjusts the tension. His arms are pulled up as his ankles are firmly held in place. Muscles scream in protest as his limbs are stretched to their limit. Just before his metal arm tears free from the rest of him, the guard stops and secures the tension. He stands back with his mates to check out their prize.

'Any idea who he is?'

The head guard shakes his head. He looks down at the handheld and scans through the data. 'Unknown male. Captain of a Nomad ship - *Ares*.' He looks at Gryffin, frowning. 'Captain? Huh. Multiple warrants. Whoa. He's been busy. Murder. Theft. Piracy. Assault. Not a nice fellow are you. What's your name?'

If they don't know, he's damn well not going to tell them. The head guard turns the lever on the chains a fraction, but Gryffin manages not to react - outside anyway. His body is screaming in pain.

'Tough guy too. What is he? Some sort of robot?'

'No idea.' The leader walks over to Gryffin and runs a finger over the top of his chest implant. He tries to pry the metal away from his skin, making Gryffin hiss in pain. 'It's in him. That's disgusting. I thought sticking him in water for a few hours would have damaged all these bits.'

'Are they still working?'

The head guard leans closer and runs his fingers along the side of his chest plate. 'Looks like it's sealed. Must be protecting whatever's underneath.' He grabs Gryffin's hair and pulls his head down. 'Huh, same with the eyepiece.' He shoves Gryffin's head back against the wall and takes a step back. 'What do you think, boys? If we keep ducking him will he rust?'

Gryffin ignores them as they laugh at the possibility parts of his metalwork will rust and fall off. These guys need to be taken down. Their arrogance is seriously pissing him off. He has no intention of hanging around so they could test their theory. They'd be waiting a long time. The metal used in his implants is rust proof - one of the few things the Scientist got right.

'That guard you killed on the transport barge was my friend. Good man. Killing him wasn't your best move. You see, you're in Tyrat until you die. Or until we decide you die. Your lifespan very much depends on how useful, how lucrative you are to us. By killing one of us you're going to be treated real special by me and my men. I can guarantee that. Only the best for you. And want to know the best part? I have all the time in the world to make you pay, a piece at a time, for what you did. In fact, how about we start right now? You rearranged his face. Only fair we do the same to you. Wouldn't you agree fellas?'

He moves outside, reappearing a few seconds later with a broken bottle. Gryffin has a bad feeling he's going to be sporting a new scar shortly. Fuck it. Whatever they do, he's not going to react. He'll shut off, head back to the safe place in the back of his mind where he spent so much of his childhood. If these bastards think they can hurt him, break him, they'll be disappointed.

'Hold him.' One of the guards holds his head steady while the other grabs his jaw, digging his filthy nails into his skin as he squeezes hard.

He digs the tip of the jagged glass into Gryffin's forehead, sending a drop of blood into his right eye. He grits his teeth as the glass slowly slices through his skin, down the top of his nose to his left cheek. Blood flows freely from the trail of red hot pain.

The men laugh and the one with the bottle receives a slap on the back from his friends. 'Little something to think about while you hang there. C'mon guys. Grub time. Let's leave no name here for a bit. Might convince him to be a little more cooperative.'

Gryffin keeps his head up and eyes focused on the guards as they pull the door closed, plunging him into darkness. He closes his eyes and lets his head rest against the wall behind him. Everything hurts. The connectors on his metal arm are agony, his face is throbbing and every joint is screaming for relief. He doesn't bother testing his bonds. Even if he did get out - which he doubts he would thanks to being stretched - the door would put a stop to any escape. The best he can do is rest while he can. They'd slip up. Cocky shits always do. Nothing pisses him off more than overconfidence. Just because you have someone in chains doesn't mean the roles can't be reversed as fast. Rafe learnt that at the expense of his nose. Once Gryffin gets out of here he'll take the other pieces of the traitor.

He gets there's a bounty on his head. There's always someone willing to make a living off the lives of others. Hell, he did it himself. He spent a lot of time and effort making sure he knew about every single bounty being offered on him. It was impossible to work out where was safe to land unless he knew whether he would be captured as soon as he landed. Because of this, he knew the bounty being offered by the prison. It was fair, but not worth getting on the wrong side of a group like the Nomad to pocket. Doubling that would have been enough of a game-changer. He can't think of anything he's done in the last two weeks since he checked the bounty. Nothing that would have irritated someone enough to go to these lengths.

He can worry about the reasons for the bounty later. First things first - get the hell out of here. He takes as deep a breath as the stretched position will allow and tries to sleep.

34

Gryffin is rudely awoken when the chains are released from the wall and he crashes to the ground in a heap of weak muscles. Stars dance in front of his eyes as pain explodes through his body. His forehead hits the rough stone floor, scraping painfully against the large cut on his face. Before he can recover from that, something freezing, wet, and foul-smelling is thrown over him.

'Breakfast is served,' the head guard announces in a sing-song voice. The unidentifiable slop drips down his neck and soaks into his hair.

The guard crouches down in front of him 'Any

thoughts on a name yet? We know you're not mute so I'm guessing this strong silent act is for my benefit. Much prefer your name though. My superiors are sticklers for details like that.'

Gryffin wipes his face on his shoulder, smearing his breakfast into his skin.

'I'll take that as a no.' He nods to his mate who steps outside. He comes back in with four guards. Each man takes the end of one of the chains and drags him back to the room with the crates. Without unlocking the chains from the restraints he is shoved back inside and the door slammed shut. He shouts and kicks the door, but doesn't make much of an impact. His body is still recovering from being stretched. The chains are tangled around his arms, making moving them impossible. Cramps he can't do anything about twist at his arms and legs, the pain nearly unbearable.

'Hey. You okay?'

Gryffin ignores the voice from the cell next to him. All his energy is going into stopping himself from kicking the door until he breaks every bone in his feet.

'Calm down. The more you struggle, the less air they'll give you.'

He closes his eyes and tries to link with the implant, but it's not keen on helping.

'You in here before?'

The conversation is the last thing he wants but if it helps keep his mind off the crate he'll bite. 'Yeah.'

'Where'd they take you?'

'Hung me up.'

The other man laughs. 'Favourite of theirs. They'll move you from the crate to the wall, then back to the crate. No time for your body to readjust in between. They'll do it a few more times to mess you up before they throw you in with everyone else.'

'They doing the same with you?'

He laughs. 'Me? No. They only do that for special guests. Don't know what you did and I don't want to know. You're on their radar though. Your time here won't be fun. Get some rest. You'll need it.'

Gryffin drops his head to the floor and does as the other man suggests. He'll need all his energy to get the hell out of here.

∞

Bray wakes with a start as the door to the crate room is opened. He hopes they're coming to let him out, but he knows it's the other prisoner they're after. He hadn't wanted to strike up a conversation, but he couldn't listen to the man's attack on the crate any longer. Probably just what the guy thought after Bray had his initial meltdown. The thing is, it didn't matter how tough you thought you were. Or even how tough you actually were. Something about the sickening confines of the cell drove even the most hardened prisoner mad.

The problem is, now he broke his own rule and spoke to the other man, he knows the guards aren't here to let him out. Whoever the man is, he's important or dangerous enough to have been put at the top of the naughty list. They'd do everything they could to break him to pieces - mentally and physically, before throwing him to the hungry masses in gen pop.

Bray's seen it happen dozens of times before and, so far, the guards have been successful every time.

He lies in the dark, listening as heavy chains are dragged across the metal floor of the crate and something large is dumped on the ground. Bray has to give the man credit. He doesn't make a sound as the guards order him to his feet and, no doubt, manhandle him from the room.

Maybe they've forgotten about him? Maybe he'd taken one step too far. Maybe, this time, the door won't open again.

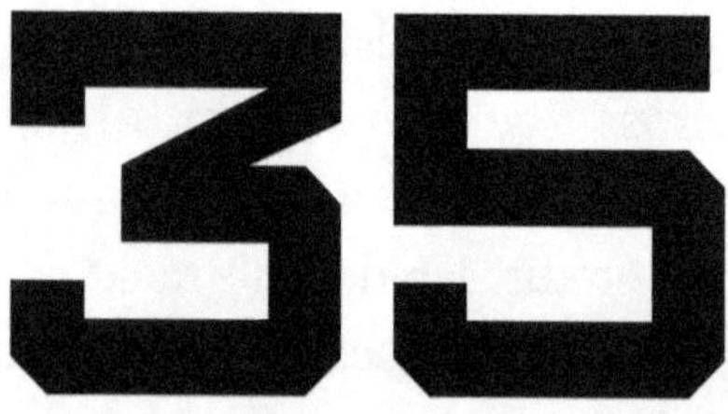

TYRAT PRISON MOON

Even prepared for pressure, Gryffin nearly passes out with the pain when he's strung up again. His implant is helping in its own special way by keeping him conscious. He looks down at the head guard, feeling nearly as much hatred towards him as he did the Scientist.

'Name?'

When Gryffin doesn't respond the guard's baton crashes into his flesh arm, just above the wrist. Gryffin hides the pain, putting himself in the same place he did when the Scientist operated on him. The pain would come later. For now, he locks it away. He feels the impact of the metal against his arm again and again until the bone finally gives, snapping under the pressure of the blows.

The interrogation continues with two broken fingers and a few cracked ribs. The longer the session drags on for, the more the guards let their frustration at his lack of response show. He watches one of them reach for the control on his chains ready to drop him to the dirt again. He's getting tired of being dropped and hung again like a trophy. He tries to tilt to the side to keep from landing on his broken arm, but he's got no control over the muscles in his legs.

He lies in an undignified heap on the stone floor as the guards pace in front of him. 'Any ideas?'

'The crate again. Longer stint. Chain him inside this time. Maybe some time in the dark unable to move will put manners on him.'

Gryffin keeps his head down as they unlock his chains from the wall. Both guards bend down to take hold of his restraints nearer his wrists. Big mistake.

Letting his implant take control, he rises to his knees. The pain from his shattered arm doesn't register as he shoves both arms back, driving his elbows into the soft tissue of each guards neck. Before either man has dropped, Gryffin pulls the metal batons from one of them. Cradling his shattered arm to his chest, he pushes to his feet relying heavily on the implant. The head guard looks at the bodies of his two comrades then back up at Gryffin. 'You've just made a big mistake.'

Gryffin holds the baton out to the side.

The guard counters by aiming his gun at Gryffin. He fires. Gryffin is aware of the round hitting his thigh, but as it's not his head he couldn't care less. He aims again, but the baton leaves Gryffin's hand before he follows through. The guard falls to his knees as the baton strikes him in the stomach. Gryffin stalks towards his prey. He stops in front of the guard and clenches his metal fist.

'My name is Gryffin.' His fist strikes the side of the guards head, ensuring the man will take his secret to the grave.

Gryffin takes a second to unlock his restraints, then relieves the men of their weapons and belts. He uses two of the belts to make a sling for his shattered arm. He grabs the leader by the collar of his jacket before cracking open the door and peering out. No alarms and no additional guards. Idiots must have thought the crate had broken him. All it did was give him more motivation to kill them.

He pauses at the door to look in the direction of the crates. Any thoughts he had about getting the other prisoner out disappear as the radio sounds on the guard at his feet. They're asking for him to check-in. Time's up.

He moves along the corridor, dragging the body with him. He gets to the door at the end and lifts the man to the retinal scanner. With only one arm it's not an easy task but he manages to hold him up while opening his eyelid. The scanner beeps and the door opens. Gryffin dumps the body on the ground and finds himself in the control room. After taking care of three guards he stands in front of the wall of screens. Each camera shows a different area of the prison. With no idea what the controls say, he turns to the last remaining guard, frozen to the spot as he stares at Gryffin. 'Open all the cells.'

'What? Are you crazy?'

'Yeah.' He pushes the barrel of the gun against the man's head and leans over. 'Open the damn cells.'

Faced with his imminent death. The man does as instructed then joins his friends on the floor. Gryffin watches as the cell doors slide back, releasing the prisoners with a roar of shouting. That should keep the rest of the guards busy.

He steps into the corridor and then ducks back inside as a guard fires at his head. He returns fire, but his aim is off. 'Fuck it.' Ignoring the rounds hitting the door, he closes his eyes and drops his hold on the control implant. He steadies himself against the wall as the room spins before his vision sharpens. The pain of his injuries eases and an eerie calm takes over. He hates giving this much control to the thing in his head, but he's dead otherwise. He'll deal with the aftereffects if he survives.

A burning sensation spreads through the connectors embedded in what's left of his right arm as the electricity builds. He opens the door and sends the burst out of his arm. A gargled scream is quickly followed by a dull thump. Gryffin steps out and looks down at the guard. The burst hit him square in the chest. He's not getting up again. Gryffin kills the comms unit under his boot and throws the weapons into the office before sealing the door again. With one hand there's no point loading himself with too many guns.

He looks over the railing at the carnage below. Guards wrestle with inmates. It's not a fair fight but no part of him cares right now. When he was brought in he was lead down which means the way out must be up. With time against him, he decides to take the direct route. With only one shot before he plummets to his death, he jumps upwards, grabbing on to the edge of the level above him. Using only his mechanical arm he pulls his body up, swinging his legs towards the railing. His feet lock on and he lets go, quickly grasping the railing in his hand before he drops. He climbs over the railing and comes face to face with four guards. He kills three but their mate gets a lucky shot off before he too falls. Adrenaline or the implant or both masks the pain of the round in his side.

Gryffin pulls open the door to the stairs and freezes. A guard is on the other side, his gun directed at Gryffin's face. The person behind the gun slowly lowers it.

'What the hell took you so long?'

Sayber drops his gun to his side. 'Hey, we just broke into a top-secret, high-security prison to get you out. Should have guessed you'd try to take the wind out of my sails by rescuing yourself.'

Gryffin leans heavily against the wall. 'Next time I'll wait in my cell.'

'I'd appreciate that. Although, can't wait to hear how you got yourself out of your cell.' Sayber contacts the rest of the team as Gryffin examines the wound on his side. 'We've got him. Fall back.'

Gryffin gestures at the gun clipped to Sayber's belt and he hands it over.

'You sure you can fire that straight? You don't look too good.'

He fires over Sayber's shoulder, dropping a guard who was getting too close.

'Take that as a yes. We've got a transport on the upper level. Probably should move our arses. You using the implant?'

'I can stretch it out another few minutes max.'

'Better get out of here pronto while you can still walk. The alarms you or us?'

'Me. Let all the prisoners out of their cells.'

'Thank fuck it's not us.' One of the Nomad with him opens the door at the top of the stairs. Another steps out, his gun raised. He gives the all-clear and the rest of the team steps out. They hurry over to a transport with the Foundation logo on the side and Gryffin is manhandled inside. He steps over the four bodies lying on the floor and peers out the front window. The docking bay doors are creeping closed. The comms unit screams to life with orders to stand down and prepare for inspection.

'Might be best you take a seat. This could get a little bumpy.'

Gryffin sinks into the chair beside Sayber and gets control of the implant. The pain in his side and leg intensifies. He presses his hand to his side as blood pours from the bullet wound.

'Right, time we make a door for ourselves.'

Gryffin jumps as the side of the docking doors erupt. 'What the hell was that?'

'Figured they'd try to keep you here so we fitted a few contingencies.' Sayber grits his teeth as the ship squeezes past the damaged doors. 'We had an epic escape plan all set up to get you out. I won't bore you with the details except to say you would have been suitably impressed.'

Gryffin smiles and lies back in the seat. 'I'm impressed, Sayber. Believe me.'

36

Gryffin curses as Ryder attempts to clean the large wound on his face. 'Sorry, sir. It's one hell of a cut. You're lucky they didn't take your eye out.'

Sayber sits down opposite him and rests his arms on his legs. 'You look like shit. You okay?'

'No.' Every inch of his body hurts. Even blinking and breathing is giving him issues. Every breath pulls on the stitches in his side. The round hadn't hit anything vital but he'd lost a lot of blood. He forces his eyelids to stay open. He just needs to hang on until he's patched up. Then he can collapse on the floor of his room and sleep for a week. 'Did they get anyone else?'

'No. When you tore off on the bike, we evac'ed the rest of the team and the guns. Found the remains of the bike in the trees. What happened?'

'Took one of the transports out and tracked down the second. Rafe had a team waiting. Few dozen men with stun guns.'

'Explains why we can't find him. Bastard's gone off-grid. The only reason we knew where you were was a rumour. Someone overheard him talking a few days before about Tyrat. We took a gamble and headed there. You see him after he sold you out?'

'He was breathing through a shattered nose. I'll finish the job as soon as I find him.'

Gryffin winces as Ryder dabs something on his face. 'Sorry, sir.'

Sayber sits opposite him and gives him a once over. 'What the hell did they do to you?'

'Tried to get information from me.'

'Failed I presume.

'Gave it a good shot.'

Sayber raises his eyebrows. 'You can say that again.' He nods to Gryffin's left arm, firmly wrapped in a heavy-duty support bandage. 'You break your arm getting out or did they do that?'

'Shock stick. Took a few hits to break.'

Sayber looks away and shakes his head. 'They did a real number on the bone. It'll need a metal pin fitted to stabilise it.'

'Fine.'

He looks down at the monitor hooked into Gryffin's

implants. 'Whatever drug they gave you is out of your system. Your implants are doing what they should. The two bullet wounds are fixable. Your face...' he looks up and grimaces. 'Not so fixable. It'll leave a hell of a scar. How did you get out?'

'I got out of my restraints, killed some guards, took the key codes and bumped into you.'

'Ah and there was me worrying you might have had a bit of trouble,' he replies sarcastically. 'How many guards or prisoners did you have to get through.'

'A few.'

Sayber purses his lips but doesn't reply. 'Sorry it took so long to get you out. We had a hell of a time tracking you down.'

'How long was I there?'

'Three days. So, as much as I hate kicking you when you're down, you want the good news or the bad news?'

'There's good news?'

Sayber grimaces. 'No. I was hoping you'd go for the bad first. The bad and only news is that your wanted report now has a name on it.'

'What?'

'Well, it was a lucky guess obviously, but you're now being identified as Griffin. Spelt the wrong way but that makes fuck all difference.'

'They cut my face, stretched me, and threw me in that... they did this to me because I wouldn't tell them my name. How the hell did they figure it out?'

Sayber clears his throat as he points to the large,

slightly beaten up, grime-covered tattoo taking up a hefty portion of his upper body. 'It's a fairly unique creature, sir. A bit of searching and they would have found a match on their system for it. Guess they just settled on calling you that. Reckon it's just dumb luck it's your actual name.'

Gryffin closes his eyes and slumps sideways against the wall. He knows the guard he told his name to died a few seconds later. Dumb luck is right. He could have just told them and spared himself the pain. He never wanted the griffin tattoo. He had wanted what all the other Nomad had. Rayde has managed to completely screw him.

'Probably wasn't a great idea to get that on you.'

'Why don't you take that up with Rayde.' He picks up a cloth and targets the bullet wound on his thigh with a pair of tweezers. The round is still embedded in his tissue but refuses to be found. He gives up and throws the tweezers onto the bed beside him. 'Let me know how you get on with that.'

'We can look into having it removed, although that won't be an easy job. Altering the design in some way might help. Ryder, is it possible?'

'Nah. The only way to hide that magnificent piece of my artwork would be to cover his chest, back and arm with a solid lump of black. Anything else, the griffin will show through. It's too damn big to disguise.'

'Too late anyway,' Gryffin says. 'Damage is done. If my name is on my record, it's out there. No taking that back. Doesn't matter what I do with my tattoo. The guards saw my implants too. I'm not hidden anymore. May as well leave the ink as it is.'

'We're not as screwed as you think, Gryffin. We just carry on as normal. Keep you covered when you go off *Ares*. Continue using the masks. Unless someone captures the whole damn crew and strips us, you'll stay hidden. Besides, escaping Tyrat while beaten to an impressive pulp will give a lot of weight to your reputation. Adding implants to that won't hurt.'

'Dangerous cyborg captain.'

'Exactly. Would you mess with a ship or a group if you thought someone like that would come after you? We're already seeing a difference since you took command. Your... how should I put it, approach on the surface has earned us some attention. Our landing parties are facing less resistance. That's a good thing.'

'We're still short of food. My reputation isn't helping that.'

'In time it will.'

'We'll be dead.'

'First things first. *Ares* is no good unless you're in her command chair. No offence but you're a few stitches, a hot shower and some shut-eye away from that. I'm afraid to ask exactly what you've got on your shoulder but it's turning my stomach.'

'Breakfast.'

Sayber makes a face. 'If you say so. I'll get you something more edible.' Sayber opens a drawer in the unit beside him, takes out a suture pack and hands it to Ryder. 'Afraid this is the best we can do for your face. We're running low on supplies.'

'Add it to the list.'

Gryffin shuffles down the bed and stares at the ceiling. Ryder holds the skin on his cheek together and sticks the needle in, but Gryffin feels nothing. He's already asleep.

37

Pain is the first thing Gryffin feels when he finally wakes up. He groans as he opens his eyes, waiting while his vision adjusts to the darkness surrounding him. He's still in the med bay, but he's alone. It feels like a fire is burning across his face. He reaches up and winces when he presses against the tender stitches. The pain in the rest of his body has eased slightly, but his muscles are crying out in protest. Hours of beatings has taken its toll, turning his visible flesh everything from an angry red to purple, to yellow. Moving is going to be fun for a while. He rolls over and takes a deep breath before pushing himself upright.

His broken arm throbs in time with the cut on his face.

Taking slow steps he shuffles across the room to the bathroom, takes care of his bladder then freezes as he catches his reflection in the mirror above the sink. If he didn't know he was looking at himself, he wouldn't have recognised his face. The guards had done a real number on him. His bare chest is a rainbow of bruises and bandaged cuts. Thick white material covers his thigh, but the blood is already seeping through. He can handle all that. Cuts and bruises are like old friends to him at this stage. It's the crude stitches on his face that bother him the most. The bastards had sliced his face in two. The line of sutures is neat but hurts like hell.

If they had more credits to buy supplies, he'd be able to equip the med bay with devices that would rule out the need for stitching his men back together again. His crew shouldn't have to settle for poor medical supplies on top of lousy rations and a ship that's out of commission as much as she runs. If they're to survive he needs to step up and change the way they're doing things.

Maybe Sayber has a point. Maybe knowing he's a cyborg or even suspecting he is, will help them when they raid. The metal, the scars, the fact he broke out of Tyrat - those things can't hurt the Nomad. Poor medical supplies and no food will.

He clumsily makes his way back over to the bed and searches for his trousers. He finally finds them in the recycling receptacle in the corner. One look at them and he decides it's the best place for them. With no other clothes in the room, he heads back to his quarters in his boxers. The first Nomad he comes across immediately stops walking and stares at him. 'Sir! Are you okay?'

'I'm fine.'

'Can I help you?'

Gryffin is about to say no when he changes his mind. 'Get me some trousers from my quarters. Bring them to the command deck.'

The Nomad nods and hurries back the way he came. At least that will save him going up an extra two flights of stairs to his quarters. The man meets him just before he gets to the command deck door. Gryffin takes the trousers and dismisses him with a nod. He leans against the wall and manages to get his feet and the legs of the trousers lined up while not falling. He pauses for a second to catch his breath then does his best to walk onto the command deck without falling on his ass in front of the crew. Using the railing, he pulls himself up to the top platform where Sayber is.

His second in command gets to his feet when he notices Gryffin approach. He hurries over and keeps his voice low. 'What the hell are you doing, sir? Are you trying to kill yourself? You should be resting.'

'I'm fine.'

'No, you're not fine. You've got a broken arm, cracked ribs, and are suffering blood loss. You should be lying down. Or at the very least sitting.'

'Get out of the way then.' Gryffin falls back into his chair and takes a few seconds to catch his breath.

'Where's the nearest colony?'

Sayber frowns. 'What?'

'Nearest colony. Where is it?'

Sayber checks the unit behind him. 'A day from our location. Maybe a little less.'

'Set a course.'

'But we're not due to land for another few days.' Gryffin looks up at Sayer but doesn't say a word. 'You heard the Captain. Let's go.'

As soon as the ship is underway, Sayber crouches down beside Gryffin. 'Sir, will you at least let me get you a shirt. Some of the wounds have reopened.'

He looks down at his chest and instantly dismisses the fresh blood soaking into the bandages. 'I'm fine.'

'Suit yourself. Care to tell me what's got you out of your recovery bed in such a hurry? I know you're not keen on the med bay but this is a little extreme - even for you.'

'We're running low on supplies.'

'That's nothing new, sir. We're always the wrong side of supply and demand.'

Gryffin winces as the stitches on his face pull at his skin. 'Not anymore. We're going to raid every damn colony we come across until this ship is fully supplied.'

Sayber raises an eyebrow. 'We are?'

'You're right. Rayde's right. We're better than this. If we can use what I am to keep food on our plates that's what we'll do.'

'I like the plan but what about the colonists. You planning on taking everything they have or sharing it around with the locals?'

'*Ares* is the priority. If people stand in our way we'll go through them.'

38

Rayde's mouth drops open when he gets a good look at Gryffin. It's only been a few weeks since Gryffin saw Rayde last but it feels like he's fought a war in that short time. Sayber had taken teams on raids while he was forced to rest – against his wishes. He'd never admit Sayber was right to ground him but he needed the downtime. He'd spent most of the four days since getting out of Tyrat in bed, trying to recover from everything his body went through. Even with the implants, he's struggling to get over it. The wounds are healing and the bones setting, but the most visible of his injuries is giving him the biggest issues. The crude scar on his face is angry, red, and hurts. The long line of sutures itches like crazy every damn second of the day which isn't improving his mood.

'So, Tyrat is as pleasant as I've heard. You look like shit, son.'

'I feel like shit.'

'Was your face injured by another inmate?'

He shakes his head and winces. 'Guard with a bottle.'

'Your arm?'

'Shock stick.'

'Do you have any other injuries I should know about?'

'Some cracked ribs, couple of gunshot wounds, two broken fingers and a dislocated shoulder. I'll be fine in a few days.'

Rayde laughs and shakes his head. 'Son, you could be on fire and you'd still say you were fine. They tortured you for information, correct?'

'They tried.'

Rayde nods solemnly. 'And what of this Rafe? I hear he pocketed quite the bounty when he delivered you on a platter. You find him yet?'

Gryffin shakes his head. 'We've got feelers out. A bounty of our own too but only with trusted contacts. He was paid with Foundation credits. They'll stand out when he spends them. It's only a matter of time.'

'Very good. What punishment you got in mind? Something fitting of the crime I hope.'

'Haven't thought that far ahead. I'll think of

something when we find him.'

'Only one suitable punishment. You need to kill him. Make an example of him. Make sure anyone thinking of cashing in on the plentiful bounties you got on your head has second thoughts. Strike hard and fast.'

'You want me to kill him?'

'Too damn right. Publicly too. People need to see what's in store for traitors.' Rayde scrutinises him. 'What's the problem, son? You've taken people out before.'

'I've killed defending myself or my crew. This would be murder.'

'And?'

'There's a difference.'

'No, Gryffin. There isn't. The result is you alive and the other fellow dead. How they got there makes no odds. Besides, I'm fairly sure you've taken out a few in training. Mighty impressive from what I remember.'

Like he needs to be reminded of that. 'I know I have to send a message but shouldn't it be the right one? I don't want people thinking I'll kill for no reason. It has to have a reason.'

'What part of selling you out doesn't give you a reason? Think about it, son. He exchanged you for credits. Foundation credits. Surely that must make your blood boil?'

'I want payback but was thinking of throwing him to Tyrat. See how he likes it. There's a bounty on his head too.'

Rayde snorts loudly. 'That plush Foundation joint ain't no punishment for betraying scum like him. Place is meant to be escape proof. Still fucking amazed you got out without any help. No, can't take any chances with him. Death is the only option.'

Gryffin stops himself before he says something he'll regret. Did Rayde really think he was treated like an honoured guest at Tyrat? He'd told him about the crates and the stretching. Did Rayde not believe him? Or did Rayde think he was weak by letting his treatment in Tyrat get to him so much? Not for the first time, Gryffin feels out of place. On borrowed time in a life he could lose with one wrong move. Rafe wasn't going to be that wrong move. 'Fine. I'll kill him.'

Rayde smiles and squeezes his shoulder. 'I know you will. Don't give him any chance to lie his way out of his mess, you hear me?'

'Yes, sir.'

'Good, now that's sorted, how about some food. The dispensers on *Ares* any better or they still churning out tasteless slop?'

'I got them upgraded.'

'Glad to hear it. Why don't you grab something and bring it back here.'

Gryffin pauses at the door and looks back at Rayde. His former captain is stretching out in the chair at the head of the meeting table, his arms behind his head and his eyes closed. Gryffin walks to the mess, but he can't shake the unsettled feeling Rayde isn't happy about him breaking out of Tyrat.

39

NAVA THREE

Rafe settles onto the stool at the bar and orders his drink. He arrived on Nava Three a few days ago but this is his first time out of the excuse for a room he was renting. The credits he earned from handing over Gryffin were begging to be spent but not yet. He wanted to make sure he was in the clear before he risked that. He'd used a little to have a doctor set his broken nose but that was it. Damn Nomad. A month on and it still hurts. The doctor wasn't the best in the Sector so he's also left with a bump where the bone didn't quite set straight.

The bartender slides the glass towards him and

goes back to his other patrons. The bar is packed - just how he likes it. You stand out a lot more in an empty room. At least if he detected a problem he could slip away through the crowd. Not that he's expecting trouble. The colony isn't linked to the Nomad. From what he can make out, the Nomad had never even visited the settlement. Maybe he'll be able to take a few weeks downtime here. Figure out where he's going to settle and spend his credits.

He orders his second drink and lifts the glass to take a sip, but the occupant of the seat next to him bumps against his arm, spilling it over his jacket. 'Hey, watch it.'

'Sorry about that.' Rafe freezes, slowly turning towards the man. Sayber raises his eyebrows as he stares at him. 'Rafe? Well, this is a surprise.'

Rafe smiles at Sayber and shuffles back in his seat, bumping into someone else. By the look of his uniform he's Nomad too. The blond-haired man raises his glass before downing the liquid. 'This the illusive Rafe, sir?'

'It is indeed. Rafe, this is Kellyn. He's very pleased to meet you.'

'I am very pleased to meet you,' Kellyn repeats with a wide smile on his face.

Rafe returns the smile but it doesn't go further than his face. Inside he's going through his options, which right now is fuck all. He hasn't got a chance of getting out of here with Sayber and this other Nomad hemming him in. He's heard of Sayber. If stories are to be believed, he's someone you don't mess with.

Kellyn also looks like he could easily break every bone in Rafe's body if he wanted to.

Sayber squeezes his shoulder and gestures to the barman. 'Let me top that up for you. Three more, please. So, Rafe, funny we should run into you here. You see, we've been looking for you.'

Rafe swallows, his throat suddenly too dry. 'You have?'

Sayber nods. 'Need some facts cleared up. Not sure if you heard but Gryffin ran into a little bother. Got arrested and sent to Tyrat.'

'Oh. I didn't hear that.' In his head his voice sounds sure but who the hell knows what it sounds like coming out of his mouth.

'You must have left the surface just after your transaction with the captain. We've heard you may have had a hand in his capture. We're not ones to believe rumours so we thought we'd track you down and get the facts from the man himself.'

'You think I captured him and handed him over?'

Sayber laughs and thanks the barkeep as the drinks arrive. 'No offence, Rafe, but I don't think you'd be up for that challenge. Hell, we wouldn't be up for it. Would we Kellyn?'

'Fuck no. The captain would kill us - well, after showing us what a massive mistake we'd made by crossing him.'

'Exactly. No, we heard you brought the guards from Tyrat to him. Told them where he'd be and when. Now, I find all that hard to believe. We've dealt with you for nearly a year. We've all come out on top from each of the transactions. Anyone the Nomad deal with is well rewarded. You'd have to be a fucking idiot to risk bringing us to your door by doing something stupid. Am I right?'

'Absolutely,' Kellyn answers, gesturing for another refill.

'So, put our minds at rest. You didn't betray us, betray Gryffin. Did you?'

'What? Of course not. As you said, I've done well out of the trades. Why would I risk that?' Rafe hopes his voice didn't come out as high-pitched as it sounded.

Sayber frowns as he studies him. Rafe wills his hand to quit trembling as he empties his glass. He needs alcohol. After a painfully long wait where his life flashes in front of his eyes more than once, Sayber finally smiles and slaps him roughly on the back. 'Told you, Kellyn. Rafe isn't the fucking idiot we're looking for.'

'I guess you're right, sir. Back to the search then.'

'Looks that way. Sorry about the questions but you get why we had to ask. Don't know who to trust in the Sector anymore. Full of thieves and liars.' Sayber laughs as he winks at him. 'Not that we'd know about that, right? Another drink to apologise?'

Rafe blows out a long breath and discretely wipes his damp palms on the legs of his trousers. 'No need, really.'

'Another round here,' Sayber shouts, ignoring

Rafe's protests. All he wants to do is go back to his room, pack his things and get the hell off the surface while he still can.

Kellyn excuses himself and wanders off into the crowd to search for the restroom. Sayber isn't doing or saying anything to worry him, but he doesn't trust either of them for one second. 'So, is *Ares* here or just you two?'

'Not taking any chances with her after what happened to Gryffin. She's not on the surface.'

Well, that's a bit of good news. Two Nomad, he can deal with, maybe. The full crew not so much.

'Drink up. Not polite to refuse an apology. You might make me feel worse than I already do.'

Rafe raises his glass, jumping slightly when Sayber clinks glasses before finishing his drink. 'Damn, that's good. Some rotten stuff out there. We were in a bar a few days ago and I swear we could have fuelled *Ares* with the crap they were serving. What do you think? Good isn't it.'

He downs his drink and nods. 'Yeah. Not bad.'

'Another round?'

'Thanks, but I think I'm done.'

'One for the road.' He nods to the man behind the bar. 'Four more.'

It takes Rafe a few seconds to realise what Sayber said. 'Four?'

Sayber smiles, but something about it gives Rafe chills rather than reassuring him. 'One for you. One for me. One for Kellyn...'

'And one for me.'

Someone a hell of a lot bigger than Kellyn takes the seat beside him. Rafe swallows deeply as the bartender places the drink on the counter and a metal hand reaches out to grasp it.

NAVA THREE

Gryffin takes the glass placed in front of him but doesn't drink it. Alcohol and his implants don't go together. He wants to be very much in control for what's about to happen. Kellyn steps up behind Rafe, caging the man between the three of them and the bar.

'I'm confused, Captain,' Sayber asks. 'Was Rafe lying to me when he said he had nothing to do with your capture or were you lying when you told me he did? What we need is some solid evidence.'

Kellyn dumps a brown bag on the bar in front of Rafe. 'Not that we doubted the captain but the credits in there say you're guilty. Found those in the room you rented. Have to say, thought Foundation credits would get you something a little more... habitable.'

Rafe stares at the bag and the colour drains from his face. 'That's not mine.'

Gryffin squeezes the glass in his hand until it shatters. He grinds the shards between his metal fingers. 'You're forgetting one small detail.' Gryffin slams his elbow back, shattering Rafe's nose again. He screams in pain as blood pours from between his hands. 'Damn sure I did that last time you fucked with me. Bad taste to taunt someone you've betrayed. Could come back to bite you in the ass.'

'Listen, Gryffin. It was just business. You know that right.'

Kellyn jabs him in the back. 'Best you call him Captain after what you did.' Kellyn leans over and lowers his voice as he speaks into Rafe's ear, 'He's not too happy with you.' He tosses Rafe a few napkins from the pile on the bar. 'You're getting blood everywhere. Sort yourself out.'

'Sorry, Captain. I'll share the reward with you. Hell, you can have it. All of it. And nothing came of it anyway. You're here. No harm done.'

'Three days in Tyrat isn't nothing.'

'What? You escaped?'

'Revenge is a damn good incentive to get out.'

He doesn't know if it's alcohol, a last-ditch attempt at finding a lifeline, or plain old stupidity, but Rafe finds his balls from somewhere. He holds a handful of napkins to his face and smiles at Gryffin, his teeth stained with blood. 'Revenge? Look around you, Captain. There must be a few hundred people here. You and I both know that sort of publicity isn't what the Nomad want or need. You have no stake here. If you stop me leaving you're going to cause a scene and piss off the leaders. So, if it's all the same with you, thank you for the drinks, but it's time I go.'

Gryffin nods at the barkeep and the music dies. Without turning to face the room, Gryffin shouts, 'Clear out!'

Rafe turns and watches in horror as every man and woman in the room obediently moves towards the exit. Not one person questions or defies Gryffin's command.

Gryffin continues to crush the glass shards under his fingers as the bar empties. 'Don't know if you've heard of a weapons broker called Hardy. This is her place. She's paying me to keep an eye on it while she's taking a break.' Without looking up he points to the door at the left of the bar. Rafe turns and curses when he sees the enormous purple griffin painted on it.

Sayber drapes his arm around Rafe's shoulder. 'You need to be more aware of your surroundings. How the fuck did you miss that?'

Gryffin pushes his drink across to Rafe. 'Drink it.'

'I don't want it.'

'I said drink the damn drink.'

Rafe picks up the glass, spilling some of the alcohol over his hand. He swallows and places the glass back on the table. 'Now what? You going to kill me?'

'Yes.'

Rafe nods slowly as he stares at the bar. 'It was just business. Nothing personal, Gryffin-'

His words end in a choked gargle as Gryffin slices Rafe's throat open. Before Rafe has taken his last breath, sprawled across the bar top, Gryffin gets up and walks over to Kellyn and Sayber. 'That all the credits in his room?'

Kellyn nods as he leans over the bar to pick up the bottle of alcohol. 'Yes, sir. It matches the bounty, minus the bit he used to pay for the room. What you want us to do with it?'

'Leave it here. It'll compensate Hardy for the mess and loss of income while we took care of this.' He looks over at Kellyn and frowns. 'That and all the drink you're taking.'

'Can't blame me, sir. It's good stuff.'

'Take some for the rest of the crew.'

'We done here?' Sayber asks as Kellyn clears the rest of the bar's supply.

'Not yet.' Gryffin looks over at the mess he left on the bar. 'Time to make a statement.'

He grabs the back of Rafe's jacket in his metal hand and pulls him out of the building. The night is warm and the street is full, mainly thanks to him clearing the bar while he killed Rafe. Plenty of people to spread the word. Rayde would no doubt be happy about that. Gryffin dumps Rafe's body on the ground in the middle of the street, puts two bullets in his head for good measure, and walks away.

EARTH

Admiral Hank Avoca refills his whiskey glass and peers out into the darkness. He's bone-weary but gave up on sleep a little over two hours ago. Drinking probably isn't the solution, but he needs something to dull the memories. Not that anything does. It's his punishment and he will accept it. He has no right to complain.

Upstairs, in their spacious bedroom with a view of the ocean, his wife sleeps unaware of the dark thoughts swirling in his mind. Unaware their lavish house and expensive transports were acquired with funds he earned by destroying the lives of innocent children. She'll never know of course, not if he can help it. It's his secret. His shame. His guilt.

With nothing else to occupy himself until morning, he turns on his work unit and sits down behind his desk. Perhaps some mindless reports will take his mind off the past - and drowning it at the bottom of a glass.

Top of the list of reports is a list of the latest inmates delivered to Tyrat. How he hates that place. The Foundation barely had a hold on the facility. It was still categorised as a Foundation penitentiary, but that was stretching the truth. The guards are given free rein to do whatever they wished to whomever they wished. Reports of arranged, illegal fights between prisoners, harsh punishments, sleep and food deprivation to name but a few, were ripe. He had brought it to the attention of the Council but they had more important issues to deal with. Who cares what a moon of thieves and murderers did?

Barely paying attention, he opens the file and scrolls through the names. Seems the Foundation security patrols have been busy. Targeting the worlds at the far borders of Foundation control was topping up the prisons. He fails to see why the Council are bothering. These people are far more concerned with the task of merely surviving. They offer no real threat to Earth or its coddled inhabitants.

He sighs and closes the file, reopening it immediately when a name grabs his attention. 'Brayden Sawyer. Now, why does your name ring a bell?'

It's probably nothing but he's not doing anything else so opens the attached file detailing the reasons for his arrest. Hank's eyebrows lift as he reads the list. Theft. Assault. Handling stolen goods. Fraud. Criminal damage. Carrying an illegal weapon. Possession of illegal substances. The list is long and, bar murder has a little of everything on it. No wonder he has been sentenced to life in Tyrat. Clearly, they don't mix in the same circles. So why is that name familiar? He checks the image supplied with the file. Tall, brown eyes, light brown hair. An attractive young man but certainly not someone he recognises.

Closing the file, he searches the Foundation system for Mr. Sawyer, finding what he's looking for easily enough. 'Born on Earth to Maggie and Dean Sawyer. Twenty-three years old.' He frowns and thinks back to the criminal record. 'You've been a busy young man. One sibling, a brother, Daegan Sawyer, deceased...' His voice trails off. He swallows, his mouth suddenly dry. Unable to move, he stares at the text on the screen, the letters and numerals blurring and merging.

Without taking his eyes from the screen, he lifts the framed picture of his wife and children from the desk and opens the back. A folded piece of paper drops onto the polished surface. In the first list of names, right in the middle, he sees it. Daegan Sawyer. The name has a red line through it with a date and some brief details in his neat handwriting. According to his notes, Daegan Sawyer died on the way to the station. He had sustained injuries during his capture that proved fatal. Hank drops the list to the table and closes his eyes. Surely this name cannot be a common one. He runs a search and the system confirms what he suspected. Only one Daegan Sawyer registered. So, this Brayden Sawyer is the brother of one of the poor souls sacrificed to the Scientist.

He retches and empties his stomach into the basket by his feet. As if the Sawyer family hadn't been damaged enough by this project. Now, Brayden was awaiting a death sentence in Tyrat. After making sure his system is hidden from Foundation checks, he cross-references all the names on the list with the inmates of Tyrat. He's hoping the Foundation isn't targeting family members of the project subjects, but after what he's seen and heard, he wouldn't put anything past them.

But there's nothing. Brayden must have been the one unlucky sibling. After he's gone through all the siblings of the project and the inmates in his report he's left with one. There's no name listed beside the Tyrat record so he opens it, just to be sure. The guards hadn't been able to get a match on the system for the man. Perhaps he wasn't born in the Foundation. Perhaps they didn't bother to check. Whatever the reason they had listed him as Unknown Male – designation Griffin. Captain of the Nomad battleship *Ares*. Quite the catch for the prison officials. The infamous captain had earned a name for himself in the last few months.

Like Brayden, his record is colourful, to say the least, but with the additional charge of multiple murders. Apparently, he began his time in Tyrat by killing one of the guards on the transport. Hank skips through the charges to the brief description at the bottom.

Late twenties to early thirties. Six-foot-seven. Hank's eyebrows raise. Tyrat's low tunnels and cramped corridors would have been especially fun for that inmate. He reads on. Dark hair and blue eyes. A large tattoo of a griffin on his chest, arm and back – hence the designation. The guards mention some unusual metalwork on his body which they describe in more detail further down the report.

Whatever feeling was left in his body after learning about Brayden, disappears when he realises this inmate has the same implants as the subjects from the project. He reads on, stopping at the line where the guard's record this unnamed inmate has a brand on the back of his left shoulder with the numerals 35 burnt on his skin. Hank checks his list again. Daegan Sawyer was the thirty-fifth subject. That means this inmate is Daegan. He reads the smartly written text beside Daegan's name on his list. That makes no sense. He was told Daegan died on the way to the station. There's no other reason for him to mark the boy off his list. He double checks the spelling, counts the names, and rereads the description from Tyrat.

He slumps back in the chair, taking some time for the information to sink in. Daegan was absolutely the thirty-fifth subject. Daegan and the prisoner in the report are the same person. He has no doubts. So why was he told this one boy had died when he clearly didn't? He finds it hard to believe the Scientist made a mistake. If the Nomad has implants he must have spent considerable time on the table. The Scientist may have been many horrific things, but he was no fool. He intentionally told Avoca Daegan died. But why?

Whatever the reason, and he has no doubts it is not a pleasant reason, one of the subjects survived. If his fellow admirals find out, they'd look for him. He's certain about that. If that happens, they could want to start the hellish project again. That can't happen. He can't let it happen.

Hank stares at the files of the two men. Two brothers separated for nearly two decades end up in the same prison at the same time. However small the odds are for such an occurrence, he is not going to look a gift horse in the mouth.

His initial excitement at having the two brothers in the same location flitters away. Daegan escaped. Hank shakes his head as he reads the sketchy details. No one ever escaped the prison. Trust the Foundation's dirty secret to be the first. There is mention of a Nomad vessel - presumably *Ares* - being seen in the area briefly before it disappeared. If Daegan is the captain of the Nomad flagship, he is safer than his brother is at this moment. At least if he's not in the prison any longer, there's one less thing to worry about. That still leaves his record though. If anyone familiar with the project learns about the brand and the implants they'll realise how important he is.

Even though it's nearly four in the morning, Hank sends out a transmission. Less than a minute later, Felix Dixon's well-lined face appears on the screen. 'You'd bloody well better be using an unlisted unit on an unlisted line with an untraceable everything!'

'I am,' Hank assures him. 'I have an emergency and need your help.'

'Of course you do. You're on Foundation Earth. It's a given you're screwed. What can I do you for?'

'I need to break someone out of Tyrat.'

Felix nods slowly as a large smile grows. 'Well, well, well. You are full of surprises, aren't you? We can meet in the usual place.'

'Tomorrow okay?'

'It's a date.'

The connection drops and Hank takes a deep breath. He's about to take a path that'll leave him in a dangerous and life-threatening place. Much like the path he took years ago when he agreed to be a part of this horror. At least this time, the path will help to redeem his previous actions. Or will as long as he can get Brayden Sawyer out of prison before he's killed.

42

EARTH

Avoca slips his glasses on as he steps out of his transport. Even though he's an admiral and considered one of the elite, he chose to live just outside the city wall with his family. It was unusual but not forbidden. He couldn't stand being in the city unless he had to be. The order, the precise positioning of everything made him feel like he was living in a virtual reality of sorts. At least out here, there was a little freedom, a little more randomness. If it wasn't forbidden, he would have moved his family to the farming region, well, what was left of it. Everywhere he goes, he can't shake the smothering claustrophobia that accompanies his every move.

Since he found the files on Daegan and Brayden he had suffered three panic attacks. Coming up with viable reasons for his wife was becoming difficult. Living a life of lies was coming in useful yet again.

He checks his watch and picks up the pace. Felix and Evie Dixon were not known for their patience. He reaches the small street-side cafe and chooses a seat against the far wall separating the business from the canal that runs alongside the road.

Mere seconds after he sits, a tall dark-haired man pulls out the seat opposite him and smiles. 'I'm Heath. I'm... looking after mutual friends. I'll bring you to them in a bit. I just want to make sure you don't have any followers.'

'How can I be sure you are who you say you are?'

'Evie got a new hat a few weeks ago. She said to say it sort of looks like the flowerbed you had at the bottom of your garden. Although without the fountain.' Heath shrugs. 'I've given up trying to figure out what that woman is talking about half the time.'

Avoca laughs and shakes his head. 'That sounds like quite a ghastly hat. I hated that flowerbed. Nothing grew in it.'

'Yeah, I've given up on trying to figure out her taste in hats too.' Heath lifts his hand and orders two coffees from the waitress. 'Hey, you okay? You look a little... peaky.'

He waits until the coffee has arrived before he answers. 'I apologise. This is a stressful situation.'

Heath sips his coffee and smiles. 'That's good. I mean the coffee – not your stressful situation.' He takes another sip and licks the foam off his lips. 'And don't worry. I'm here to make sure everyone is safe. I'm trained by the best - I'm ex-Foundation security.'

'I'm not sure if that reassures or worries me.'

Heath laughs and finishes his coffee. 'Let's go. If we're late Evie will never shut up about it.'

Avoca follows Heath out of the cafe and along the path running the length of the canal. Several less than reliable looking craft are moored to the stone wall. Some have people sitting on the top decks, enjoying the sunshine while others appear to be barely keeping above the surface of the murky canal. Heath stops at one of the more unstable vessels and steps aboard, his long legs easily reaching across the gap between the dock and the barge. He holds out his hand, helping Avoca to board then opens the shutters to the lower deck.

Evie and Felix are playing a game of cards at a wooden table that used to be pale yellow, or perhaps mustard in colour. They ignore Heath and Avoca as they continue the argument, each one giving as good as they get. Heath clears his throat and the couple finally stops their tirade.

'About time,' Evie mutters as she straightens her ghastly hat. 'Any longer and Felix would have been swimming in the canal.'

'Ha! You wish, woman.'

She dismisses him with a wave of her hand. Once

everyone is settled with a cup of tea and a biscuit. Evie nods at Avoca. 'Well old friend. What do you need our help with?'

'You've heard of Project Conscript.'

It's not a question so the Dixon's don't answer. Avoca knows they've heard of it. There wasn't much that happened in the Foundation the couple didn't know about. 'Can we presume you're involved?'

Avoca nods once.

Evie sucks in a long breath. 'What the blazes did you get yourself wrapped up in. Did you lose your mind? Have a momentary lapse of all common sense and... well, sanity. Stealing children and giving them to that man to work on. I'm disappointed in you Hank.'

Avoca laughs without humour. 'You cannot be more disappointed in me than I am myself. I am disgusted and ashamed. All I can say in my defence is that I was given little choice.'

Felix grunts. 'I'm not sure what we can do to help you.'

'I was searching through the latest convict report from Tyrat. One of the names attracted my attention. To cut a long story short, I found out this inmate is the brother of one of the subjects from Conscript. Not only that, but this particular subject somehow survived and was also an inmate in Tyrat, although he escaped less than three days later.'

Heath whistles. 'Escaping Tyrat is no mean feat.'

'Indeed,' Evie agrees. 'So, how can you be so sure this is one of the poor creatures who escaped?'

'He's a cyborg. Plus, he also had one of the identifying brands on his back. There's no doubt in my mind.'

'That is rather conclusive. So, who is this mystery survivor?'

'I was hoping you could tell me. I have a description and a connection to the Nomad, but nothing else.' He slides the handheld across the table and lets the Dixon's read the description of Daegan Sawyer. He wasn't expecting them to recognise him from his description alone so when a certain look passes between them he instantly notices. 'You know who that is, don't you.'

'Hank, this is a vague description-'

'Bollocks,' Hank snorts. He holds up a hand in apology to Evie. 'I am stressed beyond belief at the moment. I can only apologise, but I do stand by my remark. That is far from a vague description. Unless of course, you know more than one person with metal implants, because if you do we are in more trouble than I initially thought.'

The couple lean closer, mumbling to each other in hushed tones while Avoca waits, impatience threatening to release another outburst.

'Fine. Yes, we know exactly who that is, but we are trusting you to keep his name off all Foundation records. It's more than our lives are worth.'

'Of course. I'm trying to right a wrong done to him and his brother. I don't care about anything else.'

'The dim-witted guards actually got his name

correct – well, apart from the spelling. It was probably a lucky guess. I believe he has a tattoo of the creature on his chest. His name actually is Gryffin. He's the captain of a Nomad battleship. A pretty infamous one if all accounts are to be believed.'

'I can't believe he survived and rose to such a position.'

'Quite a kick in the teeth of the delightful Foundation wouldn't you say,' Evie says as she claps her hands together.

'Have you worked with him?'

'As you know, we are firmly in the grey area of society. We know of quite a few... shady individuals. I think he could be included in that group.'

'Now hang on one second,' Felix interrupts. 'You're not asking us to go after Gryffin, are you?'

'Good gracious, no.'

'That's a relief. Getting close to him will prove impossible as best. A death sentence at worse.'

'Now that I know for certain who he is, I completely agree. No, what I need help to do is break his brother, Brayden, out of Tyrat. I also need all mention of Gryffin's incarceration removed from the Foundation system and any connection to Brayden and his family severed, record-wise.'

'You think the Foundation will target this Brayden to get to Gryffin?'

'I have no doubt my comrades will do everything in their power to recapture Gryffin any way they can. Plenty of credits and time was lost when the project ended. The only consolation is that, with the destruction of the station, the project was abandoned. Knowing there's a living and, from what I can make out, successful test subject for want of a better word, they will be eager to restart. That cannot happen. I need to get Brayden out.'

'Why him? It is just because this Gryffin guy is his brother?'

Avoca shakes his head. 'Redemption of sorts. I can't help but feel he wouldn't be in there if not for my actions. Please. Can you help me?'

Felix and Evie get up and leave the room, closing the wooden shutter behind them. Avoca peers into his murky tea but cannot stomach it. If the Dixon's refuse, he is at a dead end.

'We'll help,' Felix says as he steps back inside and sits at the table. Evie nods her agreement.

'That is such a relief. Thank you so much.'

Felix holds up a hand. 'Hang on to that thanks. We're a long way from getting this Brayden guy out. The only way to access the prison is from the inside. We'll need to get someone onto the staff.'

'I'll do it,' Heath says.

Evie smiles at him. 'Oh Heath, that's so kind to offer, but we were offering you either way.'

Heath rubs a hand over his face. 'Of course. Nice of you to ask.'

Evie pats him on the knee. 'So, we have our man. We'll do a bit of wizardry on his paperwork. Make sure he fits the bill for Tyrat. It may take some time to get him in and a plan formed. I'm thinking a few months. Will your guy last until then?'

'I have no idea. He's survived this long. All I can do is hope he's strong enough.' He looks down at the picture of Brayden Sawyer. 'Hang in there – we're coming for you.'

If you enjoyed Chaos, please leave a review and tell somebody about the book. Reviews and shares are always welcome.

Thanks for your support!

The adventure continues in

MANIA

Nomad Series Book 5

Due 2021

Read on for an excerpt

1

Aleena's heart pounds in her ears in time to the intruder alarms. She loses her footing, slipping on wet leaves. Ignoring the sting of grazed palms she pushes to her feet and increases her pace. She has to reach the town centre before their unwelcome visitors arrive.

She had been preparing dinner at home when the house shook, plates and ornaments jumping from the shelves. The immense battleship appeared out of nowhere, flying low over the village - no doubt in an act of intimidation. It was proving quite effective. As the hulking form settled into a nearby field, Aleena had sounded the alarm, dispersing her people into the surrounding forest and the safety offered by the natural caves and mountains.

With no technology worth mentioning, Aleena had hoped Ultar would not attract the attention of raiding parties, and for years that was the case. She had not managed to gauge much about the vessel as it flew over her house apart from one thing as it moved away. On the back of the ship, a fierce bird-like creature glared down at her. That was enough for her to realise just how much trouble they were in. From the reports coming in from villages that have seen the ship, it is much worse than she could have ever expected. Aleena has heard many tales from travellers about the uglier side of the Outer Sector, about groups who terrorise colonies without remorse. In all her years as leader of Ultar, she was fortunate not to have met any representatives of these groups. Until now. She doubts there is a colonist in the Sector who has not heard of the Nomad. Over the last year, under the leadership of her new captain, attacks by the flagship, *Ares*, have increased in frequency and devastation. The captain is well known for storming through village after village, taking whatever he wants and leaving blood and tears in his wake. It appears their luck has just run out.

The Nomad ship, *Ares*, has arrived.

She had heard stories of the cruel and ruthless men that took what they wanted at the cost of hundreds of lives throughout the Sector. Knowing they are on her world sickens her, but she has no time to dwell on that.

She hurries to the centre of town, ushering anyone

she passes to the safety of the forest. When she reaches the open square in the centre she knows she is too late. Dozens of masked men appear from the side streets, herding her people into the town hall. She takes a step back, bumping into someone behind her. She turns and gasps when she sees a broad man wearing a metal mask. The purple lenses covering his eyes seem to glow as he looks down at her. He lifts his gun and nudges her towards the rest of her people.

'I am the leader of this world. I want to speak to whoever is in charge.'

'No chance. Walk.' He lifts his weapon and nods towards the town hall. As much as she would like to argue her point, she knows it would fall on deaf ears. Her only option is to do as she is told... for now.

ARES

NOMAD SERIES BOOK 1

(available as paperback, ebook and audio)

He wasn't expected to survive. No one else did, and for twenty years, he has managed to stay off their radar. Until now. Until her.

Gryffin was the sole survivor of The Foundation's experimental project to transform human children into hybrid cyborgs - half human, half machine. The program failed and he was sent on a one way trip into The Outer Sector where he was left for dead. He has survived for twenty years by suppressing his human emotions and embracing his machine side.

Officer Terra Rush believes in her duty to the Foundation. The Sector needs to be prepared for colonization, and nothing can stop her from doing her job...except him. When Gryffin saves her from an attack, Terra uncovers a terrible secret. The Foundation has been lying to her...and maybe they still are.

They have labelled Gryffin a killing machine, yet he acts more human than many of The Foundation's leaders. He has awakened intense feelings in Terra that throw her loyalties into question, and even though he pushes her away, she is determined to find out the truth about the cyborg program.

Gryffin refuses to be a mindless soldier, yet escaping The Foundation's control and stopping the colonization of his home will require Terra's help. Can Gryffin overcome the machine inside and trust her? Or will getting in touch with his human emotions destroy him once and for all?

NEMESIS

NOMAD SERIES BOOK 2

(available as paperback, ebook and audio)

A part of her died when she lost him.

Commander Terra Rush has spent the last eight months mourning Gryffin, believing he died when his ship crashed. When he returns to her, broken and scarred from months of torture at the hands of the Foundation, it feels like a miracle - at first.

His unpredictable mechanical side, reawakened by the brutality he endured as a prisoner, threatens to destroy him. He's lost the trust of the colonists. Has he lost part of himself as well?

Her need to protect her ravaged heart puts distance between them when they need to depend on each other the most. If the colonists are to survive, they need Gryffin to reunite the Nomad and stand with them...and he needs Terra's help to do so. But time and tragedy have changed them both so much. Can they find their way back to each other before everything they know is destroyed?

PERSES

NOMAD SERIES BOOK 3
(available as paperback, ebook and audio)

On a mission to stop the Foundation from creating an army of cyborgs, wanted felon Brayden Sawyer is trapped far from his ship and crew in the last place he wants to be...Earth. With the Foundation hot on his heels, Bray must ask his family for refuge—a family who always preferred his brother Gryffin over him and kicked him out of their lives a decade ago.

When his family rejects him a second time, Bray wonders if saving Gryffin—and completing his mission—is worth it. All his life, he's been second best to his brother, a brother he never really knew. But turning his back on Gryffin is out of the question and he won 't let the Foundation do to others what they've already done to him and Gryffin.

Breaking into Foundation headquarters, Bray comes face to face with the horrible truth about his brother's cyborg enhancements as well as his own modifications. And that's not all...the Foundation is set to destroy a planet of innocent people, using Gryffin as their number one weapon.

With time running out, Bray must finish what he started. Together with Garvan and his family, Bray must escape Earth with the necessary technology to save Gryffin and stop the Foundation's evil plans. But can one man stand against the all-powerful and tyrannical Foundation? If Bray can save Gryffin, he may just have a fighting chance.